Carrie Jan

TOXIC LOVER

*a novel*

Издательство Libra Scorp

© TOXIC LOVER, *a novel*
© Carrie Jan, *author*
© Bogdan Rusev, *translator*

First edition
ISBN 978-954-471-756-8

Libra Scorp Publishing House
2021

CARRIE JAN

# Toxic Lover

*a novel*

❀ ❀ ❀

It was an ordinary night which started just like any other recently, but it ended in a very different way.

In the middle of the night, I woke up for no reason. I opened my eyes in the dark – here I was, alone in the cold room, staring at the blackness. It was creepily quiet, I could feel icy shivers all over my body and then something caught my attention and held it fast, with its unnatural hurried beating. Yes, it was my own heart.

I lay there, waiting for something bad to happen, and suddenly the chill in my body was swept away by a hurricane, to be replaced by a heat wave, and my heart responded to it with even more frantic beating, forcing me out of bed. I was choking, fighting for each breath. I panicked and ran out into the street, still in my pyjamas. I felt my feet heavy as lead and my body paralyzed with fear as I hurried in the direction of the nearby hospital, praying that I would make it there.

I thought it was the end, but it was not.

I was fighting my fear of choking, I was feeling each beat of my heart like a hammer in my head, but still I kept running. I was sweating, the heat inside me was unbearable. Breathe, breathe, I was telling myself, the help you need is right around the corner. I crossed the last street which led to the hospital, and finally stood at reception. I tried to say something to the nurse but my lips were so dry I could not make a sound. I raised my arms, fighting for another breath of air, and collapsed to the floor.

Darkness, pitch-black darkness, and the sensation of something cold pressing against my face, a gulp of air and then another, and another after that. I sensed someone close and even though I could not see or hear anyone, I was hoping that this was salvation. I wanted to rise but I was sinking instead, trapped in the smothering embrace of the heat, and I struggled to swim up, out of the darkness, waving my arms about and crying out, or at least trying to. I was suddenly blinded by a piercing light, I blinked against it and the whiteness surrounding me, and I heard a voice.

"She's awake," the voice said.

Two smeared circles appeared above me. The shapes slowly resolved themselves into the faces of a man and a woman looking down at my face. I was staring back at them, trying to remember where I was and who these strangers were.

"How are you?" the woman asked, looking away from me at something just outside my field of vision.

I did not reply, as I did not know how I was. I was still feeling disconnected from reality.

"Where am I?" I asked in a feeble voice.

"At the hospital, you came here last night. You don't remember that?"

I did not. I could not remember, and while I was searching my mind for the memory of what I had experienced, I was seized with panic again.

"What's wrong with me?" I asked. "Is it bad?"

I held my breath, waiting to hear the worst. The nurse just touched my arm in reply, though, and then turned to the beeping machine next to my bed.

I noticed that the man with her was wearing a stethoscope on his neck. He looked at me and smiled. I read his name on the tag on his breast: Dr Steward. He explained to me that I had spent several hours in the emergency room until they had established that I did not belong there, and then I had been transferred to this hospital ward. I did not know which one it was, and I did not want to.

"You've had an intense panic attack," the doctor explained to me. "We don't know what's the reason for it – you've probably experienced a serious shock – but now that you're better, you need to keep calm and stay away from all causes of anxiety, otherwise it might happen again."

"Happen again?" I blinked in fear. "I don't want it to happen again!"

"You need to avoid strong emotions, but if it occurs again, don't let the panic get a hold of you. Take deep breaths and remember that a panic attack doesn't last for more than twenty minutes."

Dr Steward gave me a detailed explanation of what a panic attack was, and an encouraging pat on the shoulder.

"Take it easy, it's not life-threatening – it only feels like it is. And now try to sleep."

He said that it was quite possibly a single isolated occurrence, but it was not. It happened again on the next evening, when I was already back home, and on the next one after that. I was unable to deal with it by myself – neither the "buzzing bee" nor the "stomach breathing" methods helped, and the fear it was going to happen again, bringing with it the fantastical, paralyzing terror, was eroding my fragile psychological state even further. I felt like I was in a labyrinth, unable to find the way out.

I did not share the truth about my condition with many people, and John was definitely not one of them.

When I started media school, I was dreaming of a career in television, hosting my own lifestyle show. Instead, I had my own column in the evening edition of a newspaper which I was filling with comments on current political events, and – of course – I had gotten the job without applying for an interview.

I was happy to be working at all. Some of the other

graduates from my year were still going to job interviews, trying to land their first job in journalism, and they were jealous of my position, but I found it boring and lonely – even though it had one undeniable advantage regarding the hours, compared to the job of making a television show which never really ends. Knowing myself, I would not say that my current discontent would not grow even further if I had been subjected to working in the dynamic and stressful world of television.

I met John Rogers at the university where he was teaching political science, and later he became my mentor. He was a little over forty, tall and slim, with a handsome face and gray eyes sparkling like crystals, and he looked much younger than he really was. The other female students uniformly fell for him and they kept trying to attract his attention in all possible ways – some of them going as far as direct indecent proposals. John gave no sign that he was interested in any of the girls vying for his attention. He was a professional and he had no intention of risking his reputation for an ill-advised and untimely affair.

One could say that I counted myself among his admirers – with good reason. The temptation of challenging myself against such strong competition was great. But I also knew that as long as I was still in university, there could be nothing personal happening between us. I needed to wait – and at the same time, I needed to hold his attention.

This necessitated a shift in my sphere of interests – I had been planning a career in lifestyle journalism and I was really attracted to it, but it did not go well with my plan to attract John's attention, not without seeming like one of those bimbos fluttering around him looking stupid.

I developed an interest in politics and when the university website announced a competition for an article about the current political situation in the country, I saw my opening and did not hesitate to take it. The public was going to vote for the best article to be published by a national newspaper. I spent several days and nights writing, deleting what I had written and starting all over again, until I decided my article was good enough to make an impression on John, providing me with the opportunity to ask for his professional assessment. I was also expecting the opportunity to take an important step towards us getting closer. I sent him the file and I waited.

On the next morning, we ran into each other by chance. I was chatting with Sarah from school in front of the university building when John walked by, said hello and asked me to go by his office after my classes.

"He's so hot!" Sarah whispered when John continued on his way. "Even a nun's hormones would be aroused."

"Why do you say that? Are you a secret nun?" I quipped.

"You're not into him, are you?" she asked me, sharply.

"Just look at the competition you're up against..."

"There's no competition. I'm Sarah and he's going to be mine, even if only for a one-night stand!"

She glanced in the direction John had gone off to, and narrowed her eyes in a predatory way.

Sarah was so emphatic that it gave me shivers. What if she succeeded – after all, she was a sexy, intelligent blonde! This gave me food for thought.

On the same afternoon, I was sitting in John's office, listening to him talk about my article. Frankly, I had not been expecting criticism – and there was none.

"What made you take part in the competition?"

John's question was so unexpected that I was caught unprepared to answer it.

"You did," I replied, blinking at him, realizing how absurd I sounded. I hastened to correct myself, expounding on his contribution to my mature interest in serious journalism.

John was visibly flattered when he answered. "I don't teach politics, I teach art – and I can say that what you've written here," meaning my analysis, "is art. I don't know where this indecision of yours comes for, but I advise you to let it go."

"And you know something else?" John confided in me as we left his office. "A professor's greatest reward is to see his students' potential awakened thanks to his influence. You're another example for this."

I turned to thank him and in this exact moment, our eyes met. John was smiling. His proximity was provocative but I made an effort not to reveal anything about the effect he had on me. I was not able to read his thoughts, but his gaze spoke clearly enough.

I closed the door quietly and tiptoed to the bed so as not to wake John, I pulled back the covers and snuggled next to him under them. He was lying there, softly snoring. I was brimming with satisfaction. I had left all the other girls at university behind, stealing away the most handsome professor, and I felt like the chosen one.

Every single obstacle between us had been removed. I had won the competition and after that, John had taken care to land me a well-paid job with a publisher friend of his. And shortly after that, I already had my own news column. All John and I did was to enjoy ourselves and our life together. We would sit for hours talking, then we had sex, then we went into the kitchen to fix ourselves something to eat, then it was back to bed or maybe a movie. And repeat – until one of us had to go to work. It was usually John.

We had never had to deal with the question of marriage. Shortly after we started seeing each other, John just said it, out of the blue. "If you ever want to be a bride, tell me."

But I did not want to. As for the subject of "Children", it remained taboo – we both kept away from it, perhaps for fear that the other was might want to become a parent.

John proved understanding about my nightlife with the girls. After all, the substantial age difference between us necessitated tolerance for each other's interests. His hobbies differed from mine. My friends were boring company for him, and so were his friends for me. With a single exception – Margaret and Harry Taylor. Harry and John had been friends for years, and Harry's wife was almost my age, which was the reason we got somewhat close and we spent Sundays together. I was closer to Margaret than to Harry. She had presented me with a priceless gift that I loved, and it loved me back – a cute pug-dog named Poppy. As for Harry and I, we had an invisible barrier between us, and no one was willing to cross it. I sometimes wondered if the man secretly hated me, but as I could see no reason for it, I turned my back to my suspicions when they came uninvited.

It was life in the Garden of Eden, some might say – but any garden needs care, does it not?

At the beginning of our relationship, I was looking at John and listening to him with admiration – but now, a few years later, I find him tedious. Back then, it was fun to talk to him, he made jokes and I replied in kind, and then we embraced each other and laughed. But what was once dialogues is now monologues recited by him, and I can only sneak in a line every once in a while, usually out of place. My happy laughter has been replaced with a tired smile, devoid of emotion. I have come to feel irritated by everything John does and does not. I am irritated when he talks about politics, I find his pleasant politeness boring, and his concern false. We never used to argue, and now we do.

And while John was still trying to uncover the reason for my discontent, one evening a random phrase started our first argument which became our first fight.

I had already sent in my article for the day and I was lying on the couch when John came back from work and approached me.

"Bored, huh?" he said, leaning over to kiss me.

I pushed him back. "You're the reason that I'm bored!" I stood up and raised my voice as I followed John who had walked away towards the kitchen, in a determined manner. "When was the last time we did anything together, or we went out as a couple? Can you even remember?"

"Well now we're together, aren't we?" John reminded me, somewhat irritably. "And we were together last Sunday, remember?"

"No, we were with Harry last Sunday, not just the two of us. It was me, you, Harry and Harry's wife, or did you forget that?"

I was standing in front of John, almost shouting, watching him as he calmly poured a whiskey for himself and shook the ice in the glass, which seemed to take him forever.

"Look at you," I said, pointing at the glass in his hand. "This happens every time I'm here. You fill your little glass, then you drink it, then you watch TV, then you fall asleep on the couch, then you wake up some time later, mutter something, go upstairs and fall asleep once again."

"Carina, you know I'm writing a new textbook and it exhausts all my energy."

"Right, and if you're so exhausted, how come you find the strength to play tennis with friends in the evenings?"

I was shuddering with anger, feeling that I was about to lose control over my emotions.

"Come," John said and reached out to pull me closer to him.

He held me and kept me there, resting his chin on the top of my head, waiting for me to calm down. My head was against his chest, I could feel the regular beating of his heart and I let it take my anger away.

"You know," John began, "I was thinking, why don't you collect all your articles about Brexit in a book? I could help you with that. If you publish a book of your own, it would make you a significant voice in journalism."

"You mean to say I'm insignificant?" I shook myself free and narrowed my eyes at him.

"That's not what I said. I'm just giving you the idea, it's up to you to use it or not."

"Great. Now you're saying I don't have my own ideas?"

"Carina, I'm tired and I don't want to argue with you. I'm going to watch some TV."

"You see?" I screamed. "That's exactly what I'm talking about!"

I grabbed my purse and I went out. John shouted something after me, but I did not get it.

Walking on the night streets of London, I suddenly felt awful, realizing that John was, perhaps, right – at least to a certain extent. He had taken it upon himself to write a new textbook on political economy – a difficult undertaking which required his undivided attention and every minute of his time. And here I was, without any understanding for him, acting like an unstable, insecure woman. I was disappointed with myself, transferring my anger for John towards myself.

John did not have a spare minute for himself, he was always busy doing something – even when he was watching television, his thoughts were focused on something else. I reminded myself how pedantic he was, how everything was organized in a chart with him – time spent at the university, time spent with his friends, time for his hobbies. Sometimes, I wondered if our sex was organized in the same way. Once, I even made a joke about it. I noticed John looking over his schedule for the week and I reminded him to include sex in it.

"Oh it's here," he said, winking at me. "There it is, planned for Wednesday and Friday, with an encore on Wednesday if you feel like it."

But when he saw the shock in my eyes, he hurried to say it had been a joke, and he changed the subject.

On the very next day, John wrote to me as if nothing had happened on the previous evening. It was a few days before I decided to go to his place again. He sent me a message saying that he was going to come home later than usual, in case I had decided to see him. I did not yet know what I had decided, so I did not reply to him. I spent the day writing the next article and in the late afternoon, as I pressed the "Send" button, I felt relieved that I was free to whatever I wanted from now on. It was almost five o'clock. I stood up and looked outside to make sure that the rain which had been pouring over London the whole day had already stopped. I quickly dressed and went out.

In a few minutes, I was already rounding the corner of the Royal London Hospital, on my way to John's place. The streets were still wet and spattered with puddles – I was either deftly going around them or jumping over them, like a child. I was walking past people deep in their own thoughts, in a hurry to get home after another day at work, and I felt grateful that I was not one of them. I jumped over the next puddle and felt the sudden urge to cuddle with John. I had almost reached his place when I saw the local supermarket and decided to call him in case he needed me to buy something. My phone was already in my hand when I remembered that I had not taken anything else – I was in my exercise outfit and I had left my purse behind – so I reached to put the phone back into my pocket and all of a sudden – oh, no – it splashed into a puddle. I picked it up in time to see the screen slowly go black in my hands. I shook it and tried to dry it off against my sweatshirt, but the screen stayed black.

As soon as I entered John's house, I left the phone on the heater, hoping that it was going to come back to life once it was dry. I said a prayer and went out into the garden for a cigarette. But the cigarette tasted different without my phone and the internet at my fingertips. Irritated, I stubbed the cigarette out and went back inside in search of the laptop, but I did not find it and assumed John had taken it with him to work, so I went upstairs to his study where I could use the desktop computer.

I sat behind the desk, turned on the computer and glanced about the room while I waited for the machine to boot up. It was a dark place. It had been an old-fashioned library when John had bought the house, but he liked it so much that he had kept it, even though the rest of the house was gleaming in white. The room had wood panelling in dark brown; the sofa, the shelves on the walls and the heavy mahogany desk were brown, too. All of it spoke of something which had passed away a long time ago. It was beautiful once – but now it was old and melancholy.

I sighed and opened my email, but then I heard a strange buzzing sound. I thought it was the computer, but when it sounded again and again, I listened to it more carefully. The sound was coming from the desk drawer. I opened it and saw John's old phone – with the message icon showing that there were several unread messages. I was surprised that he still kept it, and even used it. He had not mentioned anything about it. I pushed the drawer closed, but then the spy in me came to life and I opened the drawer again. I took out the phone, leaned back in the chair, put my feet up on the desk and opened the first message.

*"Are you impatient yet to see me wearing black garters? I want you to ravish me while I'm wearing them."*

I laughed, thinking it was a mistake, but there was another message.

*"I want to massage you with my lips, John."*

I felt like I had been wounded in a hundred places, but I kept reading through the rest of the messages, some of which had been received on previous days.

I felt like crying with hurt and indignation. I did not know this John, and I had not expected him to betray me. Garters! John had never wanted me to wear garters.

I ran to the heater and picked up my phone.

My whole body was shaking as I switched it on – thanks God, it was working. Yes, it had survived the dive in the puddle.

I went back upstairs, used my phone camera to take a picture of the messages sent to John and, with my hands still shaking, I returned his phone back to the drawer, put mine back into my pocket, turned off the computer and hurried to leave before John had come back.

I needed time to think about what was happening.

That night, I cycled through all the feelings a betrayal can inflict. The hours spent in trying to comprehend what had happened did not manage to break me. Our relationship had become more of a business partnership than what was to be expected of two seemingly emotionally related adults, having sex every once in a while – a pleasure already devoid of feelings. Each attempt I had made to discuss our relationship had been defeated by his refusal to understand that our connection had been severed and there was a huge chasm yawning between us – an emptiness which, if not filled, would inevitably lead to us breaking apart. His ego prevented him from seeing what my emotional nature so desperately needed. I had never even noticed the change coming, as he had turned to another woman.

I decided not to tell John about the messages. In my stupor, I had forgotten to get his lover's phone number – but then I remembered I did not need to, as I had the pictures. I opened my phone and was disappointed to find out that the sender of the messages was masked behind the anonymous "X".

Before we broke up, I was going to collect evidence and have my vengeance. I was going to humiliate him as he had humiliated me; I was going to hurt him so bad he would never forget it. And then, I was going to leave, avenged.

I was not going to let the emptiness in my bed and the piercing morning silence in my house to rule over my life. I needed to change something important in my life, and let this change take me out of my depression. Antidepressants would not work, and running away from them would not change how I was feeling right now – and so, over my morning coffee, I made two decisions which might have been rash, now that I think about it. I registered myself on a dating website and bought a plane ticket to Bulgaria.

On the next morning, I was waiting at the airport.

There is nothing more boring than waiting for your flight at six in the morning. I always chose morning flights for a single reason – I could never sleep the night before, and once I was on the plane, high above the ground, I slept like a log; it was the best way to pass the time it took the plane to reach its destination.

I sat in a cafe, ordered a freshly squeezed juice and took a curious look around. All of a sudden, the phone in my pocket buzzed. I had received a message in the dating site. I glanced at the screen – one of my new friends, David, was asking for pictures. Well, since he was such an early riser, and a determined one at that, today was his lucky day.

*"Alright. Just be careful not to fall in love at first sight!"* I agreed, playfully.

*"First sight is already done, and I'm intrigued,"* he replied and sent me some "x"'s, that is kisses.

I took a careful look at his profile. I liked the manner in which he had presented himself, but even though he looked nice, he was not my type. Well, in that case I would have to take him as a temporary emotion or an emotional salvation.

My picture on the dating site was darkened and blurred, my face only partly visible, so David wanted more photos of me sent personally to him. I agreed and we swapped WhatsApp's, but then it was time for my flight and I made for the gate, promising to send him more once I had arrived in Bulgaria.

"All electronic devices must be switched off. We remind you that smoking on board is strictly prohibited."

The tinny voice of the stewardess woke me up just as I was dozing off. Her message was followed by the usual brief demonstration of safety measures – energetic gestures, emergency exits, follow the nearest line of lights, etc. It is a curious show when you are flying for the first time, but it gets boring after so many years.

My eyes were already closing when I felt the revving of the engines, the plane turned right and accelerated along the runway, to lift off seconds later. I loved the magical moment of taking to the air, but exhaustion overcame me, depriving me of this pleasure.

Five hours later, I was already sitting on the train on the way to Valentina's home village – Vodna, situated in the north-west of Bulgaria. The village was stretched on both sides of a single main street, with several small and narrow streets across.

Most of the houses had just one floor, painted sand-yellow or gray, with triangular red roofs. But they were different architecturally, unlike most English houses. The village was surrounded by sparse forest, cut through by the narrow river of Lola. I liked this place, with its cool nights and the fragrance of nature, especially in spring.

Valentina did not like it. She was born in the beautiful town called Vidin, two hours on the train away from the village her husband Gabriel is from. She did not want to live here with him and when she had come, she had thought it was going to be for a brief time only. She had told me all about her father. He was a bohemian type who had mortgaged their apartment in Vidin, quit his job and took his lover on a holiday abroad. He had never come back to them, nor had any intention of paying off the mortgage to the bank. In this way, Valentina, her mother and her brother were left without a home of their own, forced to rent. Meanwhile, Valentina enrolled in the most prestigious Sofia university for distance study in literature. She moved in with Gabriel, even though she did not love him but another man. She became a schoolteacher in Gabriels's village and later she landed another job as a schoolteacher in the nearby small town, and their family grew to include their son, Teo.

One day, Valentina of applied for a creative writing class in London and she was surprised to see her application approved. This is how I met her, one day in September, and in time we became best friends. She often visited me, and as for me, I did not say no to any invitation to visit Bulgaria – and lately, I did not even need an invitation to go. Her home was like a second home for me, and Bulgaria felt like a second homeland.

I remembered the first time Valentina or Tina for short had invited me to visit her. I had just graduated. We spent several days in the village, then we went to her beloved Vidin, where the love of her life still lived. It was a magical summer, we took endless walks, I admired the local sights just as endlessly, and we spent hours in the park on the Danube river. When we got tired, we sat on the deck of an old ship transformed into a restaurant, we ordered fish and beer and enjoyed the view over the calm water of the river. After lunch, we went to the local beach and indulged in *dolce far niente*, lying on the hot sand in our one-piece swimsuits. Sometimes we stayed out late, climbed on top of the embankment, walked slowly along the river and sat by the jetty to watch the setting sun. We told each other about our dreams. Tina wanted to become a famous writer and prayed for the miracle of Mario's wife leaving him so that he could be hers alone. She had almost made one of those dreams a reality – she had already published two poetry collections of love poems, all dedicated to Mario, of course.

My dreams were similar. I pictured myself hosting the most popular television show and a burning love for two. John and I had already went for dinner once and the evening had ended with a friendly hug, but we both felt there was more coming.

Afterwards, Tina and I went to have dinner in a restaurant, and she told me all about Mario. Finally, exhausted by the long day, we stood up with the intention of going home, but once we were out of the restaurant, Tina asked, "Are you very tired?"

And, knowing how much she wanted to hear this, I replied, "Not at all. I have enough energy left for two."

Then, hesitating, she continued, "How about we take a walk past Mario's house?"

I agreed and Tina took me down the dusty streets of the town. Once we were there, she gazed with longing at the windows of her beloved's house. We walked back around the small one-floor house and stopped by the fence in the backyard. We lit cigarettes and Tina stood on tiptoes to peer in. Sometimes, she caught a glimpse of him and she was happy, other times we only managed to get the neighbourhood dogs barking.

Tina was a few years older, but we had a lot in common. We were both emotional, we liked to share our feelings, and we sought each other's advice on everything. Everything was out in the open between us.

She was a passionate smoker, just like me; we both loved coffee and talking about men, but one of the things which connected us most was the fact that we were both depressive by nature, longing and searching for love – always in the wrong place.

The phone buzzed in my pocket – it was the alarm reminding me that my journey was about to end. The village of Vodna was not the final stop of the train and I could use a little reminder, especially on a train like the ones here, without information displays.

Minutes later, Tina was waving at me from the platform.

"I'm so glad you're here again!" she smiled happily.

I had been here only about a month and a half ago. I could see in Tina's eyes the impatience to learn what had made me come back so soon. I did not need to tell her that something had happened. She already suspected it, because she knew me well enough.

The train station was hidden away from the main street of the village, on one of the tiny side streets. The street was dusty, lined with weeds. We took it and turned onto the main street. Tina's house was almost at the end of it.

"I like this place," I quipped, took her elbow and nudged her shoulder with mine.

"Yeah, I know – unlike me. I hate it," she replied with a small frown.

"Is Gabriel home?"

"No, I'll tell you all about it."

We both took an espresso from the only vending machine in Vodna, in front of the largest village shop on the way to her house. Minutes later, we were already smoking on the small porch in front.

"Welcome!" Tina smiled, with an inviting look.

It was time to talk... and listen.

❀ ❀ ❀

"Are you still with John?"

The question almost gave me a heart attack. Maybe Tina had guessed that my relationship with John was the reason behind my surprise visit? The memory of what I had read just a few days ago flooded my mind once again. Suddenly, I could not see properly, I felt the panic rise in me and I lost my equilibrium. Tina did not seem to notice the change which had come over me. Right at this moment, I heard her say, "Here he is."

I followed her eyes and say Teo in the door. The boy with the mysterious eyes, Tina's son.

"How are you?" he asked and shook my hand.

"I'm fine," I smiled back.

I was surprised by the ease with which I lied. I was not fine at all, but there was no point in unloading the burden of my own problems on a carefree teenager.

"Sit down and tell me everything! How's it going on the girlfriend front?" I said, with a playful wink.

Teo stayed where he was. "I'm busy now, I just came to say hello. I'm making a beat, if you know what that is, but I'll have more time to talk later," he said and quickly disappeared back into the house.

"I want you to play it for me later!" I called out after him.

I turned to Lora. "So he wants to be a DJ now?"

She did not answer. She lit another cigarette and stared at me, studying my face, trying to find the traces of what was tormenting me there. There was no point in trying to postpone the inevitable. Tina knew me well enough to realize that there was a problem behind every spontaneous decision I had ever taken, and my traditional coping strategy was running away. Lora was my closest friend and just the thought that she was there for me made me feel so easy and open that I was not able to hide things from her, not for long.

"Here it is," I said and gave her my phone without looking at it. "I can't live through this again, so read it for yourself. I've taken pictures of the messages exchanged between John and a mysterious stranger with the telling nickname "X"."

Tina peered at the phone screen – first from a distance, then closer – took a nervous drag on her cigarette and then sat still as a statue. The more she read, the more furious she looked. Tina was always careful with her words, trying to be delicate and moderate, but this time she could not help herself.

"Pervert!" she shouted and put the phone on the table. "Does he know that you know?"

I did not answer right away. I leaned back in my chair and closed my eyes, trying to control my raging emotions.

"There's something else," I whispered, almost inaudibly.

"Is it pictures? Did he take pictures of himself?" she guessed, sounding indignant.

"No, or at least I hope that he hasn't. Do you remember Margaret? His friend Harry's wife. I found out they've texted each other and met as well, without any of them telling me about it. They've spent hours together and he was thanking her, saying that the time he's spent with her has been "unforgettable"."

"And you're friends with her!" Tina said, openly indignant now. "See, this is yet another proof that you can never trust a man – it's his hunter's nature, he never sleeps. So what are you going to do? Are you leaving him?"

"No. I'm going to keep an eye on him."

"And why are you going to torment yourself in this emotionally masochistic manner?"

I could not avoid this conversation, but I knew a way to put an end to it – for now.

"I need food as well as love to survive," I said, changing the topic abruptly, but in a soft voice. Plus, I really was hungry.

"God," Tina said and leapt out of her chair. "Look at me! And you're my guest!"

She dashed to the summer kitchen. I did not follow her – it was our tradition that I let her prepare dinner by herself on the first evening we were together.

Nothing had changed in the years since I had first come here. Darkness had imperceptibly crept over the village. The main street, where Tina's house was, had grown especially quiet and still. There was no life in the village once it was dark – people spent their evenings in front of their television sets and only the lights in their windows showed there was anyone around. A dog barked somewhere, and others answered. A strange calm came over me as all my problems started to seem very far away, as if they had nothing to do with me.

My senses were tingled by the smell of barbecue. I reluctantly stood up. When I went to the summer kitchen, dinner had been served – the kebab, meatballs and chicken on a spit, traditional for Bulgaria, served with fries and cabbage salad. Teo appeared, grabbed his dinner and disappeared again. Smokey, Tina's cat, was circling the table without making a nuisance of himself. I gave him a piece of my kebab, he snatched it out of my hand and hid under a chair.

Perfection. I always felt at home in this place. Even more so, since dinner was so good. Lora and I kept chatting as we ate, and then retreated to the bedroom, both of us trying to keep to everyday topics. As it often happened, we returned to the memories of moments we had shared – some carefree, others funny, a few sad. We both still kept the child alive in us, always ready to do something crazy, but tonight we did not let it out. Remembering was comforting.

I woke up after ten on the following morning. I had slept through the night. Tina and Teo were certainly gone to school by now. The sun was already bursting through the blinds, flooding the room. It was going to be a warm, dry October day. There was a note on the nightstand by the bed: *"Breakfast is in the summer kitchen. The bar on the main street has the best coffee. Tina."*

I was not hungry, but I could use a fragrant refreshing coffee. I took a shower, dressed and went out of the house straight onto the main street, then I took a right turn and in a few minutes, I was already having my first coffee. At this time of day, the place was busy. A car stopped in front of the cafe and several young people got off, talking loudly. There were two mothers on the next table, discussing domestic issues – or at least that is what I thought, judging by the few words I could translate for myself. Their children were gobbling sweets, exploding in a game of tag every once in a while. I liked this carefree atmosphere. In this place, no one was in a hurry to get anywhere, there was no public transportation and people walked or rode their bicycles everywhere; a few had cars. I relaxed, leaned back, crossed my legs and lit a cigarette.

But the otherwise fine day had something unpleasant in stock, as well. I had not spoken to John in two days. He did not even know where I was. I had switched off my phone once I had arrived in the village, and now I had to switch it on. I needed to.

I ordered a second coffee. I lit another cigarette. I dialled the familiar number and it rang once, twice, three times before it went to voice mail. I cut the connection without leaving a message.

I was asking myself if John had even noticed my absence when the phone vibrated in my hand.

"What happened?" John asked, sounding confused. "Where are you?"

"In Bulgaria."

"Where? What are you doing there? How come you left without telling anybody? You have obligations! How is this irresponsible behaviour even possible? How would you feel if I did something like this?"

I was quiet. My stomach lurched. If there had been a way to avoid this...

"Carina?" John shouted. "What's wrong? Just recently, everything seemed fine, and then it suddenly changed, and you're leaving for Bulgaria without a word. Speak to me!" John insisted.

For a second, I felt like hanging up on him, but then I said, "I need change and I want to be away from London, from you, from work. I need to think, John, something has to change. I've never felt so lonely. I'm tired by life, I need something new, some pleasant thrill."

"Stop it, this is ridiculous! I don't want to listen to you."

There was a brief silence, then John timidly asked, "Is this your way of telling me that you're leaving me?"

I thought about the dating website. Was it right to search for another man if my relationship with John was not over yet? Was I not betraying him in this manner? Why could not I simply ask him about the messages and demand an explanation? The decision had already been made, somewhere deep inside of me, and I was not going to change it.

"No, I'm not leaving you."

"*For now,*" I added without saying it aloud.

"Alright then. When are you coming back?"

"In a week," I replied, uncertainly.

"Oh, I just remembered. Last night, you didn't send the article for today's edition of the newspaper. Peter was mad that he couldn't get a hold of you. Since none of us could find you this morning, either, I sent him one of your articles you've written on my laptop. Peter said it will do the job."

I did not thank him. I thought about John, always able to find a solution, never in any hesitation or doubt, always making the right decision.

❀ ❀ ❀

After a week of carefree life and positive emotions, rainy London was quick to meet me with a reality check. One of the reasons that I wanted to go home was Poppy, my friend in loneliness, who was waiting for me there. He was the dog that Margaret had given me as a gift. My father was supposed to bring him back to my apartment today, after a week of exile in their garage, as my mother had asthma. I could not wait to hold him, and it looked like our joy was mutual. Once he was in my arms, Poppy whimpered in happiness, poking me with his nose and tapping on my body with his front paws.

"Did you miss me much, my friend?"

In reply, he gave me a wet kiss on my chin. I petted him, then I took my phone out of my purse. The tension in my belly was back. I felt hot and stifled. I stood up and opened the window. I filled my lungs with the fresh night air, breathing it in again and again, struggling to keep calm and fight off the rising panic. I tried to focus on my senses but I could not do it, as the fear was overwhelming me. In a few seconds, I was already in the kitchen, a pill against panic attacks in my hand. I swallowed it and slid down to the floor, waiting for it to take effect. It would work in just a few minutes, a few brief minutes more. Breathe, slow and deep, breathe...

I hated this condition – the doctors had repeatedly assured me that it was just a temporary discomfort, quick to pass and not life-threatening, but experiencing it was still scary. Once it came, it took control of you. The pills were my only salvation – they worked every time.

Half an hour later, lying with Poppy on the couch, I noticed that I was still clutching my phone. I had forgotten about John, and I needed to call him – but just thinking about it brought a nervous tic to my face. I glanced at the phone display – it was too late to call, so I just texted him: *"I'm home."* His reply was instantaneous: *"I'll come by tomorrow night. Good night!"*

I did not know what I had been expecting, but this message left me sad and disappointed. I felt lonely, unwanted and unloved. I nudged Poppy who was in my lap, but he did not react – he was sound asleep, hardly noticing anything around. The pill was in full effect now, and as I dozed off, I remembered the blissful look on Lora's face when she was with her beloved man.

I had heard a lot about Mario, I knew how he looked from his Facebook pictures and Tina's personal archive, and I had even seen his silhouette in the window when we spied on him from the fence surrounding his back yard, but we had not really met until the other day. I realized that I was prejudiced about him, and meeting him in person left me with a mixed bag of feelings. Tina's many stories about their relationship had built up to the image of a man I could not dislike. I remembered the dozens of times he had brought her to the brink of the abyss with his indifference and opened wounds in her soul with his cheating, only to bring her back to himself with a single call, as if he was wielding a magic wand instead of a phone. All-forgiving Lora, driven by that madly intoxicating love for him, threw herself back into his arms every time, filled with uncontrollable desire. Hers was not just a passion, it was an addiction, a dependence that she could not – or maybe did not want to – control. She was going to sleep and waking up thinking about it, it was the oxygen she was breathing, the blood running through her veins. She was fully committed to this love, she had made it the purpose of her life.

And this was totally not good for her, with a man like him.

I could see her hands shaking with emotion when she dialled his number, her eyes shining with excitement when they arranged to meet, I had seen her waiting with trepidation for the moment in which she was going to be in his arms – if only for a few stolen hours or a single day. Even though it was secret, this love was inspiring and heartfelt. I secretly prayed for a breathtaking love in my own life. It could be a forbidden love, as long as it was joltingly passionate.

My phone would not shut up. Whenever it stopped ringing, the messages started coming in. I looked around – I was still on the couch, but there was no sign of Poppy. I needed a shower, some food and strong coffee, and then...

Oh, yes – how could I forget what came then. Then it was time for my gray and boring everyday life, with the tedious task of writing yet another article. Hmmm, I needed a hobby – why not a couple of them, in fact. I might buy a camera and take photos of Poppy chasing squirrels in the park during our walks. That would be interesting – but come to think of it, I could take another look at the dating website, as it might prove more exciting.

After a cup of coffee, I turned to the task of checking my missed calls. John was the first – he was sorry that he had forgotten I had a dog, so he could not come because of his allergy, and did I mind going to his place instead? Nice Margaret was asking me how it had been in Bulgaria and when we were going out shopping again. I did not remember telling her about my plans, so it must have been John. What had the two of them been up to, together, without me knowing about it? Were they lovers? Was she the mysterious "X" from John's messages? I deflected her invitation for the time being... and I did not find her so nice anymore.

My mother was the other caller who had dared to disturb my sleep. But no, I was not going to spoil my day with her. I was going to call her in the evening, when I was already with John – she was only spare with her words and criticism when I was with him.

My boss. With him, it was the sooner the better, so...

"Hello, Peter!" I said, without waiting for a greeting. Peter was not the kind of man who spends time on niceties.

"Carina, I hope your article is finished and sent to the editor's email address already?"

"No, but it will be there within the hour."

"If you want to work for *Evening News*, you can't be late."

That was it. Peter hung up. No "Goodbye", no "Have a nice day", no nothing. I was not surprised – it was Peter Addams, after all. Nice guy.

I was just about to start daydreaming about him when his name appeared once again on my phone display.

"Did you forget something?" I asked, somewhat sheepishly.

"It just occurred to me that since you've been in Bulgaria anyway, I want you to write an article about the country – and the next time you're there, bring back some photos. You need to move away from Brexit, I want more colour, more scale. Diversity, Carina, diversity!"

And that was it, again. The man of my dreams. I exhaled.

Sarah. Sarah? What did she want now? The last time we saw each other was two years ago. Since then, we had confined ourselves to birthday and holiday greetings on Facebook. After we graduated, she landed a job as a journalist, just as I did, and just recently, she founded one of the most popular news websites in England. Her efforts were to be admired. We arranged to meet. I could not wait to see her.

Tina. I smiled, thinking about last week. I texted her a few lines and promised to write again after I had seen John.

It was David's turn. He wanted to meet me for coffee tomorrow and invited me to his place afterwards. This was interesting – he was not wasting his time. I accepted the challenge and then concentrated on writing yet another article on Brexit.

It was past seven o'clock in the evening when I rang John's doorbell.

"My dear, welcome!" John stepped back to look at me, then he gave me a second look. "You look well. I hope you're feeling well, too."

"Yeah, I'm fine," I replied, hesitating. I felt like asking him about the messages, the anonymous "X" and Margaret, but I had decided to find out the truth on my own, so I simply lied. I had been doing it more and more recently, but it was better than having to endure the false sympathy in people's eyes, followed by tedious questions.

"Why didn't you use your own key?"

"I wanted to avoid surprises."

I smiled at John's back.

He stopped for a second on his way to the kitchen, but he walked on without turning back, as if he had not heard anything.

If someone ever asked me if I had any hobbies, I would not hesitate to answer, "Yes, eating."

John had prepared the best lasagna I had ever tasted. And while he was eating slowly, telling me about the events which had occurred while I had been absent, I was already getting a third helping. In about an hour, John stopped talking, laced his fingers together and rested his chin on them, looking at me in a thoughtful manner. I thought it was time for politics and I made a joke.

"Don't start talking before I've switched on the recorder on my phone, I need information about my next article and I can't miss a priceless source like you."

I made to stand up from the table to get my phone, but John caught my hand, very serious.

"No politics tonight, I promise."

For a moment, we looked at each other. Then John reached for his glass of wine, slowly raised it, swirled the wine inside and put the glass back on the table without taking a sip. It was a ritual of sorts that he practiced on the rare occasions when hesitation tried to find some way into his soul – but he always managed to regain his determination before the person sitting opposite could sense the lurking doubt.

"I think it's time you get a second job."

"What?" I raised my eyebrows and opened my mouth in surprise.

"Yes. A change would do you good. You'll be much more engaged. You could create your own news website and hire some contributors, or start writing for other publications. There are numerous opportunities – don't let yourself drift along with the current but try to control your own path instead. I can make some calls."

"Wait a minute!" I said sharply, interrupting John's speech. How dare he talk to me in this casually condescending manner?! "You don't mean to say that I can't take care of myself and I need your help, do you?"

"I mean to say that if you need to share something or hesitate about what decision to make, I'm always here for you. You don't need to dash off to Bulgaria every time you feel uncertain of yourself – problems are not solved there but here. Running away is not a solution – the solution is change. You need to be strong and determined. I advise you to take Sarah's offer, whatever it is – some additional commitment can only be good for you."

"How do you know about Sarah?"

"She asked me for your phone number – I assumed it was something to do with work."

I did not say anything, as I knew John was right. He was always on the right path, he always knew what he wanted and he was purposeful – something that I was not. He found it easy to get the right balance in any situation and approach people in the right way.

"Come," John said, interrupting my thoughts, and gave me a look which was an invitation to go to bed. Then he stood up and held my shoulders. "I can't wait to taste you."

I shivered and I sensed that my anxiety was ready to mount another attack on me. I suddenly pictured his lover, dressed in her sexy silk underwear, with a lustful inviting look on her face. I stood up abruptly and looked around for my purse. There was my salvation.

❀ ❀ ❀

I did not have to wait long. David arrived on time at Rainham Station. A black sports car with tinted windows slowly pulled up next to me and I got in with a smile which was quickly replaced by surprise.

David was not the David I had been expecting to see – at all. He was about twenty to thirty kilograms heavier and about ten years older than the man in the photos he had uploaded to the dating website. He looked like Jabba the Hutt – a monstrous body mass spilling over his car seat, with a large round head with two slits for eyes looking sheepishly at me.

"Uh, h-h-how was the t-t-train?" he asked me, stuttering.

My surprise was replaced by a moment of shock and I thought about getting off the car and leaving, but then my curiosity got the better of me.

"It was fine, for rush hour. Is it far from here?" I asked, as the car slowly left the station behind.

"N-n-no, it's f-f-five m-m-minutes a-a-aw-w-way," David kept stuttering, visibly embarrassed.

We continued the drive in absolute silence. I was watching the buildings we passed by, and David was watching me. I could not see him, but I could feel his eyes traversing my body. All of a sudden, I heard again the particular "Uh" he greeted me when I got in the car, so I turned and looked at him.

"Yes?"

I smiled, still wondering what I was doing here and why.

"You're v-v-very b-b-beautiful. B-b-breathtaking, l-l-like," the fat man declared and showed me his crooked, slightly yellowed, protruding front teeth.

I thanked him, but I could not force myself reply with the same compliment. I stared at him, hoping to find at least one attractive thing. He was wearing a faded gray t-shirt and dirty jeans that must have been blue once. Driving with one hand, he suddenly found the courage to reach out with the other and take my hand. Oh, my, I thought – well, I had wanted a challenge and here it was, sitting next to me, sweating and grunting. I was fully expecting this huge mass of flesh to spill over any minute and drown me on the spot. The thought of this gave me the shivers and I considered telling him to make a U-turn and drive me back to the place where he had picked me up, but I had not faced this particular challenge before – going on a date with a stranger – and my curiosity decided to take the risk. Plus, he might turn out to be a man with a kind heart, looks could be deceiving... yeah, right, in this case only a blind person could say that.

"We're h-h-here," Jabba grunted.

I looked around – we were turning into a small side street, then we stopped.

The house was old and unattractive, with a stone staircase without a railing. We took the stairs up to the first floor where David's apartment was. He opened the door and invited me to enter the dark corridor first. I took a few steps in the darkness and I stopped. A weak, blinking light was coming from the end of the corridor, probably from a television screen. I was hit by the heavy smell of moisture and mold, mixed with cigarette smoke. David closed the door and stood behind me; I could feel his heavy breathing and I bristled with alarm. I knew David's last name and I had seen a photo of him standing proudly next to his daughter and his car, with the car registration plate clearly visible. I had sent the details to Lora and I had explained to her where I was going before I left. Just in case, I had also told Judy – one of my childhood friends whom I had been avoiding since my panic attacks started. Lora was familiar with the man's profile on "Meet Me", as well – and she was the only one who knew the whole truth about my acquaintance with him.

"Switch on the lights!" I told David, turning back to face him.

"Uh, it's m-m-more r-r-romantic in th-th-the d-d-dark," he refused, gently pushing me in the direction of the blinking light. "W-w-we d-d-don't need l-l-light, we'll c-c-cuddle and w-w-watch a m-m-movie."

"Cuddle" – it sounded so revolting that even my stomach clenched.

For some reason, I continued down the corridor, slowly as a blind person, trailing the wall next to me with my hand, and after a few steps, I reached the room with the television. I paused in the darkness for a few seconds, waiting for my eyes to adjust. There was a large kitchen table with no chairs in a corner of the room and another table, low and long, in the middle. The coffee table was heaped with DVD's, cables, a few phones, a pile of newspapers and countless other things. A large plasma-screen television set was switched on in silent mode, in the back of the room. There was a huge corner sofa facing it, with a dresser on one side, sporting a bowl of fish. A portrait of a little girl, probably his daughter, was staring at me from the wall.

"My d-d-daughter," David announced proudly, following my gaze. "She's v-v-very b-b-beautiful, isn't sh-sh-she?"

"How can I see her in the dark? Switch the lights on!" I insisted loudly, suddenly aware of the whole absurdity of the situation.

"It's f-f-fine. S-s-sit down."

He took my hand and pulled me towards the sofa. I noticed the open windows and felt a little better.

"I'll p-p-put on a m-m-movie," David said and bent over to pick up the remote control from somewhere under the sofa. "D-d-do you l-l-like it?" he asked, indicating the screen.

"Which movie is it?" I asked even though I could not care less, glancing at the television.

"*The B-b-beauty and the B-b-beast.* It's a good one, we c-c-can c-c-cuddle while we w-w-watch."

"Can I smoke here?" I asked, adding to myself that Carina the beauty was about to eat him alive if she did not have a cigarette.

"Y-y-yes," David allowed and disappeared in the door behind the fish bowl. He returned without an ashtray, however, rummaged about under the sofa and came up with a chipped plate instead. "Uh, u-u-use th-th-this."

I asked myself what was the appropriate moment to leave on a first date, aggressively pulling on my cigarette. It seemed that my lungs were not prepared to take on this amount of smoke, I choked on it and I started coughing. David was just sitting there, staring at me.

"Wateeer!" I managed to croak out, and David disappeared behind the fish bowl once again, while I was fighting for breath and my eyes were filling with tears. But even with the tears, in this dark room, I could see well enough the dirty glass of water he stuck in my face.

My stomach lurched, I leapt up and tried to switch on the lights in the room. There was something sticky on the switch which transferred to my fingers, but the room stayed dark.

"Where's the bathroom?" I turned to David in horror.

He was still hovering next to me, looking confused.

"Th-th-this way," he said and dragged me down the dark corridor, with an open door at the end.

"Switch on the lights immediately!" I commanded. I saw David reach in front of my face and pull on the string hanging from the ceiling. I noticed the sink and tried to run the water.

"It's n-n-not w-w-working, t-t-try th-th-there."

I turned and saw David pointing at the shower above the bathtub. I grabbed it and the shower head was left in my hand. I desperately looked at David and he turned the faucet. I washed the nasty stickiness off my hand, took a deep breath and returned to the living room.

"Ten more minutes, then I'm off," I declared.

Then I sat back down and lit another cigarette. David was sitting next to me, smoking and grunting.

"Say something," I urged him, hoping to break the silence.

"Y-y-you have v-v-very b-b-beautiful eyes."

"What colour are they?" How impressive – I doubted he could see them in the dark.

"L-l-light coloured."

"Yeah, you're almost right. They're blue," I replied. I watched the pictures changing on the screen of the silent television set, then I felt an arm slowly snaking around my shoulders and pulling me to him. I turned and saw David's face dangerously close to mine. The smell of cheap perfume hit me so hard I felt sick again. David closed his eyes and puckered his lips forward, going for a kiss, and I abruptly pulled back to escape this passionate impulse. My cigarette was out in the plate, the ten minutes were over and I needed to put an immediate end to all further attempts at intimacy, so I quickly stood up from the sofa and announced, "I need to leave. Will you drive me back to London?"

"Y-y-yes, are you e-e-ever c-c-coming b-b-back?" David asked hesitantly, grabbing my hand.

We looked at each other, outlined against the dancing shadows of the scenes featuring the Beauty and the Beast, and even though I knew the answer, all I said was, "We'll talk about it later."

I sidestepped around David and went back out on the street, feeling a little calmer, and minutes later we were back on the way to London.

"So how was the date?"

I heard Tina snickering on the other side of the phone, then the click of a lighter and a long puffing exhale. She was smoking – I could picture her holding the cigarette between her lips and letting out the smoke, squinting her eyes and frowning, like she always did whenever she was concentrating on something. I regretted not being in Bulgaria. I felt so relaxed there, with Tina.

"Tell me!" she insisted.

"Never again! No dates with strangers from dating websites, that was it for me."

"It's good you didn't meet a rapist or a killer! And it's strange that you didn't get a panic attack. Perhaps, subconsciously, you judged him as a harmless one... And thanks God, that's what he was indeed. I can't believe such slobs exist at all! He asked a woman to his home and he doesn't even have proper lighting, let alone a romantic dinner waiting? Well, there was something romantic – the movie he chose," Tina concluded after she listened to my story. Then she lowered her voice. "I'm facing a similar challenge myself."

My conversation with Tina lasted longer than my date with David. It was not just two good friends talking – it was a therapy session which always left me with a smile on my face. With Tina, everything was emotional and fun; her keen sense of humour brought sunlight to the most clouded day and presented even the most alarming situation in a comical manner.

"Really, never again," I said to myself, entering the password for my profile on the "Meet Me" dating website. While I checked the users who had seen my profile and opened the messages, Poppy was pacing the bed, searching for the best place for a nap. I had about twenty unread messages waiting for me. I opened the first one and started reading the proposal.

*"I checked your profile and now I want to add something about myself that I haven't put down in mine. I am a responsible man with a sense of humour, elegant, lively, educated, proactive, cultured and in the know. I am a very direct man. I am a hedonist. I detest bad manners, vulgarity, coldness. I am companionable, I am divorced, I don't have kids. I am a lawyer and I'd like to meet you. Do you think that will be possible? Kisses."*

Oh, my, what a parade of "I"'s. And this Narcissus thinks that I am good for him?

Really, never again.

❀ ❀ ❀

I woke up in a cheerful mood, even though it was a gloomy morning outside the bedroom window. I glanced at the clock: it was almost nine. It was Friday which meant that John did not have lectures at the university – at this time of day, I could always find him in the kitchen, enjoying his first coffee and the obligatory review of the news. I thought about going there and spoiling his morning idyll. Although I was seriously considering breaking up with John, I could not say I found it enjoyable that he preferred to make his erotic dreams come true with someone else instead of me. It had not only hurt me, but also made me angry enough to dissipate any feeling of guilt that I had.

John was making it so easy for me with these messages of his. I could stick the phone in his face and tell him that I knew everything, I could play the role of the deceived, deeply hurt woman, I could rage and even shed a tear because of his betrayal, even though this would be over the top and not my style. In the end, I could turn around and slam the door closed in unfaithful John's face, and then leave with relief because it would not be me putting an end to a relationship which had lasted for years.

I got up and began to dress, already engaged in a dialogue with the cheater in my mind, pouring accusations down on him, when my phone rang. It was Tina. I picked up and did not give her a chance to say a single word.

"I can't wait to end it with John today!"

"Wait, you don't need to hurry," Tina calmly advised me, "let's see how far he goes. Wouldn't it be better to know who she is first? If it was me, I would find out who she was before I did anything else."

"I'll force him to tell me!"

I heard the familiar puffing sound from the other end of the line. Lora always did that when she wanted to get some time to think before she replied – taking a long drag on her cigarette and slowly, slowly exhaling the smoke, frowning in concentration. I imagined her and a small smile played on my face.

"So what are you suggesting?" I asked her.

"You know that men wouldn't admit they're cheating even if they're caught in bed with no underwear on. I don't think John will be an exception. If there really is someone else, you'll only make it easier for him by leaving. You could wait a little bit longer. Where there's no feelings, there's no pain," Tina concluded in a philosophical manner.

In spite of all the boredom this relationship was filling me with, I decided to listen to Tina's advice. Behaving like this, John was throwing the shadow of doubt over my own sex-appeal, in which I had no doubt myself in any other circumstances, and he was also provoking me to search for the answers to questions I would have never even thought about asking before this happened. If I was going to make him happy by leaving, I was prepared to stay a bit longer – even if our relationship was getting crowded.

"Still here?" I asked doubtfully over the phone. We had been silent for so long that I thought Lora might have hung up.

"Yes, I still haven't told you why I called."

"Something with Gabriel?" I asked in a whisper. (I had picked up this habit in her place.)

"I'll tell you when we see each other."

"And when's that going to be?" I cried out in excitement.

"Be ready to have me for Christmas."

"How many days is that? I want to count them."
"It's just a few weeks."
"I have so many things to tell you..."
"So do I."

Already dressed and wearing make-up, I was going down the stairs when my sense of smell registered an unfamiliar fragrance which became more tangible when I turned towards the kitchen.

"Good morning!" I said in greeting even before I had seen John – I knew from experience that he was going to be there.

And I was right – with a small exception.

"Good morning!" two voices replied in unison.

I looked around, surprised. John was not alone. A vaguely familiar man stood by the kitchen door leading out towards the back garden of the house. We stared at each other, clearly surprised to see someone else in the house. I had no idea anyone was coming and I did not know who he was, but I was certain I had seen him somewhere else before, even though I could not remember where and when.

John did not make an effort to introduce us which went to show that it was all business between him and the stranger, and it need not concern me. They went out together in the garden and left me in the kitchen by myself.

I did not usually have breakfast, so I made some coffee, took my cup and went outside in front of the house to have my morning cigarette. Normally, I would smoke in the back garden, but it was not available this morning and it would have been inappropriate to go there, especially since John could not stand cigarette smoke.

I was shivering in the cold, finishing my second cigarette and feeling oddly excited, when the front door opened and the stranger came out, followed by John.

"Goodbye," he said to me in passing, leaving behind the mysterious fragrance I had detected in the house.

John walked him to the door of the garden where they continued to talk to each other. The stranger stood facing me and I had the chance to get a good look at him. He was a tall, big man with gleaming black hair and large, dark eyes. His swarthy skin gave him an Arab look. He had a deep, husky voice, somewhat nasal, like someone with a cold. There was something in his appearance which turned me on. I shivered again, probably with the cold.

"Who was that man?" I asked John as soon as I walked back inside.

"The architect I hired for the extension."

"What extension?"

John gave me a serious look.

"I've been telling you for months that I want to pull down the outside wall of the kitchen to the back garden and build a glass extension in the garden connected with the house, which will make the kitchen larger."

John planned for the new extension to be entirely made of glass, including the roof.

I had forgotten about John's plans, plus I thought the whole project was pointless – even more so because it would make the small garden disappear.

My nostrils once again caught the scent of the architect's perfume – this time I managed to recognize the fragrance, it was bergamot. The smell was intoxicating and seductive.

"So he'll be coming back?"

Busy leafing through the morning paper, John did not reply.

It was past noon when I sat down in a particularly

tiny restaurant in Covent Garden. It was a narrow room with the tables so close to one another that it was all but impossible to sit without your chair pushing against the next table. Sarah had chosen the restaurant because of the food, and she was a woman of good taste, so I trusted her choice.

"Do you like it here?" she asked me.

"It's claustrophobic, but I can survive if the food is worth it."

"The food is fantastic," Sarah assured me once again. "It's a lovely place, you'll want to come back."

I took Sarah in – she was beauty personified, impossible not to like. Both men and women found her irresistible. She left them speechless and breathless. She was not only beautiful but intelligent. She had an infectious enthusiasm which hit everyone around her like a virus, enchanting them to do whatever she wanted them to do. She could direct what everyone around her did, effortlessly. It was a real pleasure listening to her – and this is exactly what I did while we had lunch.

Sarah had created one of the most popular news websites in England. She sounded enthusiastic when she described the work of the website for me, as well as the advantages of online over print media; she told me how interesting and fun working for them was, how you are always facing new challenges and you can get feedback by following the readers' comments under your articles and responding to them, if you want to.

"So, to put it briefly," she summarized at the end, "I'm offering you a full time job, eight hours a day, the choice to work from the office or from home, responsibility for national news and of course, if you want to participate in that, international news."

Sarah's offer sounded attractive and it was presented

with such enthusiasm that anyone listening to her would have responded with a quick, determined yes. Me too, but I restrained myself for two reasons – one, it would be unprofessional of me, and two, a full time job... well, it was not for me. Especially now, when my mental state was clamouring for attention.

Sarah interrupted my thoughts. "I'll be happy to work with you. I'm always interested to read your articles and I'm sure our readers will like you as well. I can't wait for you to say "yes"," Sarah said with a conspiratorial smile. "I'll give you one week to think about it, no more. I need people and I don't want to lose my time setting up job interviews when I know you."

I promised her that I would think about her offer and be quick to respond, even though I already knew what would be my decision.

"So how's lovely John?" she asked, switching to personal topics.

"Still devoted to his work. And what about you? Did you find your prince in shining armour?"

"I have so much to do that I don't have time to go looking for him. You're very lucky to have John, you know. Some day, I'll certainly be with someone like him – handsome, intelligent and invariably positive."

Sarah was talking with a dreamy look, staring at something in the street outside.

This was Sarah, alright – first the work, then everything else.

"I hope you find your John soon," I told her, sincerely. But I meant the one that we both thought we knew – and not the lying hypocrite he had become.

It had been pouring all day over London, but the rain had finally stopped. While I was dressing to go to John's, I was feeling a mild tension – a sure sign that the next panic attack was around the corner. I thought about driving there, but the fear that I might be behind the wheel with nowhere to park when I felt sick was enough to put me off. It had happened once before, and my greatest desire had been to stop the car in the middle of the street and rush on foot to the nearest hospital. Luckily, I had quickly found somewhere to park, but I could not trust my luck every time. The memory of this experience was still too vivid and I chose the thirty-minute walk to John's house instead.

I walked out equipped with a bottle of mineral water and a pocketful of pills, even though I knew that they could only help me to postpone the crisis, and not avoid it completely. I was never able to deal with this challenge without chemical aid, and in spite of the doctor's and psychologist's advice, I invariably preferred the easy way out, with the solution ready in my pocket. I checked the contents of my pocket once again, just in case, deliberating for a second about sparing myself the unpleasant experiences by staying home and spending a relaxing evening by myself, but then the desire to go out proved stronger.

It was seven in the evening, and John was still not home. Sitting in his warm kitchen waiting for him, I began to feel the effect of the drugs. My eyes started closing on themselves, so I stood up and moved to the living room which was cooler. I sat down on the couch and let the calm envelop me in its pleasant embrace. Then I sensed a familiar scent. I took a deep breath and the aroma seemed to fill my entire body, feeling like a fresh breeze. I sat up and sniffed the air again. Bergamot. I was not mistaken, everything around me smelled of bergamot. He must have sat on the couch, I thought, and then my eyes were drawn to a folder on the table in front of me. It looked familiar.

Yes, I thought, jumping up as if I had been hit by an electrical shock – it was the folder the architect had been holding this morning. I reached for it, picked it up and held it close to my face before I inhaled – here is where the fragrance was coming from.

I felt my stomach tighten with excitement. I took a deep breath and opened the folder. It was full of architectural plans and notes. It was his, no doubt. Thrilled, I opened on the first page: A.V. Architecture and Design. My eyes focused on the office address, I gasped, grabbed the folder and sprinted to the kitchen for my laptop. In a minute, I was already sitting in the garden pavilion, more awake than I had ever been.

I could not believe my eyes: his company's address was right in my neighbourhood, on the street next to mine, and Google Maps showed me a white house on three floors. Was it where he was working? I held my breath as I wrote his name in the search engine – the search returned profiles in various social media, but it was more important for me to find his picture, so I started clicking on pictures and looking at them, but – nothing, in a few more minutes of scrolling up and down the screen, I sighed in disappointment. I checked all social networks – still nothing. The profiles with photos were not his, and the ones without photos remained a mystery.

A.V. had a profile in LinkedIn. I clicked on it hopefully, expecting to see the manager of the company, my eyes slowly went over the laconic information provided in his profile, and I was just about to decide there was nothing there to tell me if he was the manager of the company or not, when my eyes grew wide with disbelief. It was an evening full of surprises.

I glanced at my watch – it was past nine which meant that it was almost midnight in Bulgaria. Lora might be sleeping, but my curiosity was wide awake and looking for answers, so the message saying "It's important, call anytime!" was sent.

Right at this moment, John appeared in the doorframe and gave me a sullen look. "How can you enjoy sitting out in the cold and smoking?"

"I'm enjoying my last days in this oasis you're determined to turn into a glass box."

"You're successfully turning it into a smoky desert," John offered sarcastically.

"Where were you?" I asked him, sensing it was not an appropriate time to try to learn more from him.

"In a cafe with Harry, and I'm exhausted. It's late, baby, let's go to bed."

"I'm not ready to sleep, and I have a lot to write yet," I lied.

John stepped closer, held me by the waist and smiled gently when he bent over to kiss my lips. "Don't stay up all night."

I checked my phone – Lora had not called yet. I tried once more to find something online about the sexy architect named Daniel Vasilev, but I still got nothing. I returned to the couch and tried to sleep, but every time I closed my eyes, my imagination offered me erotic scenes featuring this exciting man. I looked around, and for a moment, I felt ashamed about lying on John's couch, in John's house, and cheating on him in my mind. I felt my face flush, but then I remembered John's dirty messages and I decided there was nothing wrong with dreaming a little, filling my head with sinful thoughts and wishing for them to come true.

My emotions were stronger than sleep. No man had ever managed to steal my sleep, but here was a complete stranger who had succeeded in that. I wondered if I was attracted to him or it was just curiosity – that powerful female curiosity which makes you employ all weapons in the arsenal of attraction to attract a man's eyes. It must be curiosity, what else could it be, I was telling myself, turning this way and that on the narrow, uncomfortable couch.

"You're already missing me, huh?" Lora sounded in a playful mood.

"You'd better tell me who you spent the night with?"

"Why are you asking that?" Lora said, feigning surprise.

"Well, you sound like your night has been full," I laughed.

"Ha, it was full of fantasies, more like. You'd better tell me what's so important to keep you up all night."

"You'd better see for yourself," I replied and sent her the message I had prepared.

"You're not wasting time. There's even a link. Is it a picture?"

"No," I replied laconically.

I lit a cigarette and heard the familiar click of the lighter on the other side. It was a ritual of sorts we both engaged in when we were talking on the phone.

Then, there was a long silence on both sides of the line. I was holding my breath, waiting for Lora's reaction when she finally saw what I had discovered on the previous night. If it was confirmed.

"Are you sure this is the right man's profile?" Lora asked me, seriously.

"Yes, I'm almost sure. You can never be one hundred percent sure of anything. But I'm looking at this company's project, and this is the name of the manager."

"He might have been a representative of the company."

"No, he's not. From what I overheard him and John talking about, I was left with the impression that he's the company manager."

Lora was quiet for a while, then she said, "His name is Bulgarian, he graduated from a Bulgarian university, he must be Bulgarian. Now you only have to ask him to confirm it in person. What a coincidence, huh?"

"There's something else," I said in a hushed voice, as if I was about to reveal an important secret.

"What is it?" Lora asked curiously.

"He's my neighbour, living on the street next to mine, or at least that's the address of his office on the documents."

"So what are you waiting for? Hire an architect."

"Oh, yes, I do have some designs for us," I chuckled quietly.

"You never know where love might be waiting for you..."

❀ ❀ ❀

I went home but I could not stay in one place. My curiosity kept nagging at me and I decided to take a walk to the neighbouring street. It would be a great coincidence if I were to meet the object of my interest, but it was worth a try. As soon as he noticed that I was holding his leash, Poppy understood a walk outside was in the cards, and began to whimper with pleasure.

"Come on, Poppy!" I called out and opened the door. It was enough to make him wag his tail happily and dart by me and in the street outside. He already knew the way to the park and he sprinted ahead, but when he saw me turning in the opposite direction, he paused and barked a few times in the direction of the park.

"Not today, Poppy!" I called out to him and continued on my way, determined. The pug-dog hesitated for a moment but then it quickly followed me.

The street that Daniel lived on was small and narrow, consisting of about twenty row houses. The house that I was looking for was almost at the end of the street. I already knew how it looked as I had checked it on Google Maps, so I recognized it immediately – the only thing I did not know was what floor he lived on. This was what I had come to find out.

It was an old Victorian house with a small garden out front, like all the others in the street. I crossed to the opposite sidewalk to have a look at it from a safe distance. I noticed an old couple fidgeting around a kitchen table through the window on the first floor. I could cross it out from my list of suspects.

I turned my gaze higher up. There was a faint light filtering out from behind the drawn curtains on the second floor. The third floor was dark. I looked around once again and noticed Poppy exploring the front yards of the neighbouring houses, so I quietly called out to him, but he only glanced at me and continued on his rounds. I stepped up to him and managed to grab him just as he was trying to crawl under a garden gate left ajar. I carried him in my arms and we crossed the street together. I was happy to notice that the old couple on the first floor was already seated at the table, with their backs to the window. I looked both ways and I left Poppy down by the garden gate, then I nudged him lightly to go inside the garden, thus providing me with the perfect excuse if I was caught inside. But Poppy failed to comprehend my intentions and once he found himself free of my embrace, he ran in a semicircle, deftly sneaked past me and ran off to explore the neighbouring houses.

I did not have much time, so I summoned all the courage that I had and quickly made for the front door of the house where the bells were mounted. I had just taken a couple of steps when the outside lighting came on. It startled me and for a moment, I thought about going back, but then my curiosity got the better of me, and a few seconds later, I was already reading the names on the bells. I was not wrong – everything I had found out about Daniel on the internet was confirmed, except for the fact that he was on the second floor. I turned, calmly walked back out into the street and continued on to my place, satisfied with a mission well accomplished. I threw a glance at the little traitor running around and realized he needed some good training. The only word he understood and reacted to, like a soldier to a command, was "food" – in everything else, he was rather wayward.

I was not in the mood to spend the evening or the night by myself, so I left Poppy hungrily eating his dinner and went back out. I took my car and drove to Belsize Park.

Ten minutes later, I was in my parents' living room. Dad was lying on the couch watching a football game, and he sat up to give me a kiss; then, like he always does whenever he is watching something interesting on television, he hurried to send me off to my mother in the kitchen.

"You're going to eat dinner, aren't you?" my mother asked and began to set the table and serve the food without waiting for an answer.

"I'm not that hungry."

"I can see you're in a good mood," she added in a sly manner. "You need to eat so that you can make your good mood last longer."

"And what if I'm in a bad mood?"

"Same thing," she replied and put my dinner in front of me. "You eat to get your good mood back."

"Go on then, eat," she urged me. "You'll tell me all about it later."

Then she started browsing through some cookbook.

In this house, eating was a holy ritual and no one was allowed to disturb the eater unless it was to offer more food. And this was always done in a whisper.

While I was eating, my mother was leafing through her book, glancing at my plate every once in a while. I recognized her impatient look and I knew she was waiting for me to finish my dinner so that she can start interviewing me. It always happened like this when she had not seen me in a week or two, and whenever we saw each other more often, I was given the role of the listener while she talked.

"Do you want a cup of tea?" my mother offered when she saw me standing up from the table.

"I'd like a coffee."

"At this hour?" she said, surprised. "You're not going to some club again, are you?"

"I'm not going anywhere, I'll spend the night here."

My mother turned abruptly and gave me a very confused look, and I gave her a sly wink in reply.

"Has John asked you to marry him, then?" she asked, handing me the cup of coffee.

"Why do you say that?"

Dad, who had meanwhile entered the kitchen, paused to hear what I was going to say in reply, but then he saw my amazed expression and went back out without a word.

"Why not, you've been together so many years, he should have asked you a long time ago. Do you have another boyfriend, then?" my mother tried to guess again.

"Does it have to be something for me to be in a good mood?"

"Yes, it does. What's this John thinking, anyway?" my mother said, warming up to her favourite subject. "How come he's not asking you to marry him? Does he think he's going to last forever?"

My mother had never approved my relationship with John, pointing out the serious age difference between us. She thought I needed a husband and not a father.

"You already have a father," she reminded me once again, beginning yet another harangue against John.

The more she talked about him, the faster her words came, and her voice kept rising in pitch. She always mentioned his age first before she went on to describe what she saw as disrespect on his side by not asking me to marry him and leaving me no choice but to become an old spinster. This happened each time my mother decided it was time for me to marry, or she learned of someone else getting married.

"All my friends married off their children and now they have grandchildren. I only have one child and I'm not able to enjoy having grandchildren at all!" my mother moaned.

I sometimes thought that she cared more about the missed opportunity to take care of grandchildren, like all her friends did, than me being an old spinster.

"It's not that you should marry an old man," she continued, in high gear, "but to have such a beautiful woman by his side and not ask her to marry him? He's all old and grizzled and he's still waiting to do it!"

She continued with a list of John's flaws, speaking ever more quickly. Soon, she would be forced to raise her hand to her mouth as she fought off a bout of asthmatic cough, and it would end the verbal outpour.

I stopped listening to her. My thoughts took off in another direction. I thought about Tina's words that you never know if love is not waiting for you around the corner, and they seemed prophetic now. Around the corner – quite literally.

John happened to mention to me that the architect was going to arrive by bus to see him tomorrow.

"Maybe he'll get a taxi," I guessed, trying to provoke John into sharing more with me, but he did not say anything in reply to my comment.

I saw an exciting opportunity to meet Daniel, seemingly by chance, and it was enough to light my imagination on fire with visions of the next morning at the bus stop I guessed he was going to use to get on the bus to Swiss Cottage.

I spent a sleepless night considering and reconsidering every detail of our dream encounter. I carried out an infinite number of dialogues with Daniel in my head, writing them all off as too bland. It needed to look like a meeting by chance. A casual encounter.

I was not good at pretending, so at the end of the night, I decided to improvise with whatever the situation presented me.

If it was an ordinary morning, I would have been still in my bed, but I had an emotional meeting to look forward to and I could not sit still, so at six o'clock I was already up and standing in front of the coffee machine, smoking cigarette in my hand, waiting for the fragrant liquid to give me the dash of freshness and boldness I needed the most at this moment.

A little later, I impatiently opened my wardrobe and chose a thin wool dress which accentuated each curve of my body, an elegant wool coat in violet and knee-high stiletto boots – extremely uncomfortable to wear but worth it when the goal was to impress a man's eye.

It took me about half an hour to transform the broom on my head into a decent hairstyle and apply make-up. I looked at myself in the mirror from every angle and I was left happy with what I saw.

The rest of the time I spent listening to music. At ten to eight, I smiled for the last time at my image in the mirror and a minute later, I was already walking purposefully in the freezing December morning. Under the awning of the bus stop stood a few women huddled in their heavy coats, and when I approached, they gave me an apathetic glance and retreated back into their own thoughts.

I stood with my back to the bus stop, gazing in expectation at the street Daniel was supposed to come from, and I waited. I stood there smoking, the cigarette smoke was slowly dissipating into the icy air around me, the cold was seeping in through my clothes and I was shivering slightly.

Half an hour passed, I saw several buses come and

go, my feet began to hurt from staying on the same spot and I began to pace up and down without taking my eyes off Daniel's street where I still could not see anyone coming. It was almost nine when a kid on a scooter appeared around the corner, chased by several screaming children and two mothers walking in a hurried manner, probably their mothers; but there was still no sign of Daniel whom I was expecting with such impatience.

In my disappointment, I supposed that he might have taken another route or perhaps called a taxi. It was pointless to keep waiting, but I lit my next cigarette nevertheless, telling myself I was going to wait until it was finished and then, if Daniel was still not here, leave at last. I took one drag on the cigarette and felt sick, so I threw it away, disgusted. The pleasure of smoking was gone, along with my good mood. I looked at my hands, frozen stiff and puffed from the cold, and hid them in my coat pockets. My body was shivering, reminding me of the absurd situation I had placed myself in. All of a sudden, I was shaking so hard that the last remains of my enthusiasm evaporated.

I took one final look around and did the most sensible thing I could do after my insensible act – I made for my place, though I took the route by Daniel's street, of course, in a last desperate attempt to run into him.

"Sensible?" I said to myself, puzzled. "Sensible has nothing to do with it."

I sat in front of the heater turned all the way up, shivering under a thick blanket. I was already feeling the first symptoms of an onset of cold attacking my body. All of a sudden, my mind was flooded with questions – and the answers were making me feel extremely pathetic.

It seemed that my frozen body had frozen my mood, as well. I was sitting there with my head on my knees and an empty look in my eyes. There was no reason for me to feel this way, but then again, I was experiencing a sensation of emptiness inside me, and any psychologist worthy of the name would have told me that my life was in crisis. And I would have agreed. Yes, my love life is in crisis. I urgently need love.

I was startled by the phone ringing. I hesitated and reluctantly pressed the green button.

"This is no good," I heard in the *Evening News* editor's bored voice.

"What is no good?" I asked irritably, even though I guessed what he was talking about.

"Your last article. I can't run it – it's all facts and no analysis. I want it fixed within the hour."

I tried to object but he had cut the connection. I glanced at the phone in my hand once again to make sure that no one was going to hear me, then I screamed into it, "Fuck you! And fuck this!"

The heavens were raining their displeasure on me. I clenched my teeth and swallowed back the impulse to cry, and it was good that Poppy stepped into his bowl of water right at this moment, spilling it all over the floor, because it helped me to focus on something else and stopped the coming tears. I might have not been in the mood to write at all, but I had no choice – and my editor knew it. It took me exactly an hour to rewrite the article and even though I had the vague suspicion that I might be repeating an old analysis, I sent it off. I might be wrong or I might be right – and if I was right, I was hoping that no one would notice. Right now, I did not much care if Peter and his cohorts were going to love it or not.

All I wanted was to sit around and feel sorry for myself, but today was the last day of the week Sarah had given me to think about her offer. I reluctantly dialled her number.

"Hello!" I said hesitantly. "If you're busy..."

"Oh no, no, no, I'm not taking no for an answer." My telling uncertainty had been registered by the perceptive Sarah and she had the upper hand. "Why are you still working for that unscrupulous guy? Peter would never offer you what I'm offering you. If you have a problem with the working hours, consider it settled the way you want it to be. All I want is to get fresh articles from you on a regular basis."

"It's not just the working hours. I want to write about society events, not about politics."

This was the job I had been dreaming about since I was in the university, and now I saw the chance of realizing my dream, even though I expected objections.

"But political analysis is what you're good at." Sarah had been expecting me to say no and she was not able to conceal her surprise by the turn our conversation had taken.

I did not reply and she did not say anything more, either. I knew that she was using the silence to consider my offer. Her fragile looks were hiding a stubborn and determined nature – qualities which had she had to thank for her success. Sarah would never accept anything which did not satisfy her completely, and she always found a way to get what she wanted. It did not matter if she was going to purr or bite – what mattered was that she had the prey in her grasp at the end.

Sarah knew that my free spirit would often make decisions instead of my good sense, so she offered, "Start with politics and when you can, write for the lifestyle column as well, I'm not going to limit your output. But your experience in politics is too valuable for us to throw away," she kept her ground. "No limits on your work, Carrie," Sarah tried to convince me, knowing how important it was for me to avoid all restrictions and limitations preventing me from realizing my full potential.

"Alright," I agreed testily, even though I knew that the freedom Sarah was giving me would only go as fas as the length of the leash she was holding.

"You can start right away, but I'm sure you'd want to do it after the holidays, so I'm not going to insist."

"A new year for a new beginning."

"Just as successful as the previous one," Sarah wished for herself.

"Let's hope so," I replied uncertainly, with a touch of sadness.

"Less hoping, more doing! You should know that I don't work with pessimistic people," she said, then she laughed. "I'm joking."

We both knew that she was not joking.

When the phone reminded me of itself once again at half past seven, I knew it was John this time.

"How are you, darling? I'm afraid that if you don't come right away, you're going to have dinner alone."

"That's what I'm afraid of, as well," I agreed gloomily.

"Are you alright?" John asked me.

I wondered if I had heard a touch of concern in his voice, and if the concern was for me or his own self.

"I think I've got a virus."

John tried to make light of it. "A computer virus?"

"A human one," I replied irritably.

"Do you need anything?"

"Just to sleep."

"Go on then, go to bed and we'll talk again tomorrow," he replied.

I was ready to swear that I heard him sigh with relief.

"So, what happened with the...?" I began, uncertainly.

"With what?"

"The project for the kitchen. I thought that in the morning, you were supposed to have a meeting with..."

"Oh, that," John interrupted. "We postponed the meeting until after the holidays. They won't be able to start work before the beginning of March, anyway, so there's no hurry."

Stood up, was the first thing which came to my mind. I had been stood up, waiting for someone to come for a whole hour in the freezing morning outside. I quickly said goodnight to John and cut the connection.

I lay back on the couch and closed my eyes. I was like a castaway on a desert island, completely overwhelmed by the emptiness inside me. If I was feeling anything at all, it could be summed up with the words "sorrow deep beyond description". I did not have what I needed and the horizon was still unclear and covered in mist.

On the next morning, I woke up groggy. I stayed in bed, trying to clear the fog in my head. The antidepressants and sleeping pills I had taken on the previous day were still keeping me relaxed and the warmth in the room did nothing to dissipate my desire to stay in bed even longer, enjoying the illusion of calm. I knew that it was just a temporary condition which was soon going to disappear without a trace, and in just a few hours, worry and tension were once again going to go toe to toe for control over me.

The phone alarm startled me and my foggy mind slowly yielded the image of Tina waiting for me at the airport.

"Oh no!"

I leapt out of bed, grabbed the phone which had already stopped ringing and looked at the time. It was five in the morning, and I had three hours to get to the airport. I tossed the phone on the bed and dragged myself to the kitchen. Now I needed another kind of stimulant to neutralize the effect of the sleeping pills. I quickly gulped down a large cup of coffee, filled a thermos for the drive, got dressed, put my hair up in a loose bun and hurried to leave my sanctuary.

I got in the car and took a determined turn into Daniel's street, driving slowly. When I approached his house, I bent over the steering wheel so that I could see the windows better. They were dark. *"When will I see you again?"* Thinking that, I felt a pleasant thrill in my stomach. I smiled at the silent house, had a sip of coffee, lit a cigarette and, feeling somewhat fresher and calmer, drove to the airport. The streets of London were still quiet at this early hour, but if I did not manage to leave the city quickly, I would be stuck in morning traffic.

I expected to greet a sad Lora in need of cheering up, but she was in a lovely mood. We made short work of a cigarette each, standing outside the airport building, then we walked to the parking lot.

"Well, tell me all about it!" I urged her as soon as we got in the car and took off on the way home.

"No, you'd better tell me. Did you find out anything new?"

I did not need her to tell me twice. Over the next hour, making my way through morning traffic, I did the most selfish thing by unloading all of my emotional baggage onto Lora's shoulders. I told her everything, down to the last detail, and Lora was her usual patient listening self, and when I mentioned that I was considering a visit with a psychologist once again, Tina was quick to reply, with her legendary wit, that I did not need any "psychologist". I was feeling happy that Tina was here when I parked outside my place.

"Wait a minute, let's have a smoke outside, I've been sitting for hours, I want to feel the London air."

"Alright," I agreed and passed her the pack of cigarettes.

Tina hit my sore spot by saying, "I don't understand why you're hesitating and postponing it so much. Why don't you just call Daniel and invite him to your place? A house always has something that needs fixing, doesn't it? You can think of all kinds of reasons to meet him, and then it will be just the two of you, you can talk, you will show him that you're not indifferent to him and if he doesn't get the hint, you can tell him directly."

"Yes," I said with a sigh, "everyone makes choices and then has to live with the consequences."

"What matters is that you have the opportunity to make a choice. If it was me, I would have called him by now and asked him to come." Tina winked at me, just like old times, we looked at each other and burst laughing.

"And there's nothing stopping me from doing that now," Tina kept talking. "After a glass of whiskey, I'll have the courage for the first call, after the second I'll have him say yes to a date with you, and after the third, you can be sure I'll bring him straight over and into your bed."

"Let's keep it to two glasses then, what do you say?" I replied in jest.

Tina gave me a searching look, just to make sure that I meant it, then she slowly moved closer to me and asked, in a conspiratorial manner, "When?"

"When you have your repertoire ready."

❀ ❀ ❀

I checked coat and jacket pockets, shook out the contents of purses, I finally checked in the car – nothing. I could not find the flash drive I kept my latest articles on. I must have forgotten it in John's laptop. I thought about calling him but then I remembered that he was out with a friend this evening. I started the car and drove to Swiss Cottage, but I passed by Daniel's house first. The windows were lit, telling me he was home. I smiled and continued on my way.

I no longer had any desire to discover the identity of the woman John was cheating on me with, nor the duration of the affair, nor even why it had started in the first place. It would take effort to learn more about his flame, and I had no emotions to spare.

John had never looked at another woman and he had never given me a reason to be jealous. None of us had any doubts about the other, we had a steady and sometimes boring relationship. It suddenly occurred to me that he might be looking for the least painful way to part with me. Were they discussing it, him and his lover? Were they feeling sorry for me?

The siren of a fire engine passing by yanked me out of my thoughts, I turned into John's street and I saw lights in his house. So he must have returned home – or perhaps he had not gone out at all.

I entered, quietly closed the front door behind me and listened. It was unusually quiet; I made for the kitchen but I had scarcely taken two steps when I heard John's voice from the second floor. I stopped and looked up. John was not alone – I could hear him talking with someone else in his office. Slowly, holding my breath, I started climbing the stairs, and when I was several steps away from the top, I heard John's voice once again.

"I insist that you leave immediately!" He sounded determined, and also a little threatening.

A chair creaked and a familiar bass voice replied, "I'm sorry, but I can't do that, not until we figure things out. I don't accept your decision – I can't accept it. We've passed through so much, we've been together for so many years, even before you met Carina. And now, all of a sudden, you're making a decision without discussing it with me. You've decided by yourself, alone!"

The calm in his voice was quickly replaced by growing desperation, and that is when I recognized him – it was Harry, Margaret's husband. But what was he doing here and what was he talking about? My whole body tensed and I paused, lurking on the stairs, praying that someone would not come out and find me eavesdropping on them. I had no idea how to extract myself from this situation, but my growing curiosity held me fast in place.

"Alright," Harry continued, sounding resigned. "Let's not do anything rash, let's give ourselves some time. A month or maybe two, what do you say? Together, we can go over things once again, and then..."

"I don't understand why you're refusing to comprehend what I'm telling you!" John replied, irritably. "My decision is final, that's it!"

"That's right, I refuse to accept this decision, and I think it's time you told the truth to Carina! If you don't, I'll do it, to spare you the awkwardness."

"No!" John cried out. "Don't you even dare getting Carina into it."

"Isn't it too late for that? It was not me but you who got her into it, and I can't see a reason for not telling her."

"Never! I'll absolutely never let her find out, and

don't you dare interfere – you or Margaret or..."

My heart was thumping so wildly that it threatened to burst out of my chest; my ears were ringing with the tension, as if a freight train was passing through them, and I could hear John's voice but I could not understand what he was saying. I thought I was going to faint. I had no idea what they were talking about, but I was certainly involved in something that I was not going to like. Icy shivers ran over my body, as if the freezing January air had crawled into the house and was threatening to overcome me. I swayed in place as the signs betraying the onset of another panic attack threatened to smother me at this most inconvenient time. Right at this moment, I heard Harry talking once again.

"Or what? Are you threatening me? Is there another woman?" Harry kept with the questions. "There is another woman, isn't there? Or maybe it's another man? Is it?" His voice shook with fear and helplessness.

I was frozen in place on the stairs, and the coming panic attack threatened to drive me away.

"Our society is full of gay couples now, and no one is shocked when you tell them you're gay. Gay couples are getting married, John – and you're still worrying about your reputation."

"Do we really have to go over this once again? It's boring – leave, please."

"It's boring... I'm boring you?... Do you love her?" Harry asked, sounding almost hysterical.

"Stop it!" John screamed, and I thought he was going to come out of the room and see me any moment now, but no one appeared.

"It's not Carina, is it? You don't have anything to offer to her anymore... Who is it?"

"It's not your business what I have to offer to her, or not."

"You told me yourself that sex with a woman causes you psychological damage, didn't you? And now..."

Harry did not finish, as it was suddenly quiet, then I heard steps and the armchair creaking when someone sat down. The silence was so complete that I could hear my galloping heart. I was not able to move a muscle or take a breath. No one was talking now, and I prayed that no one would come out. My hand was hurting and it was only then that I noticed I was clutching the railing on the stairs too hard, so I slowly eased my fingers open and I let it go, careful to keep my presence unnoticed.

"Leave." This time, John's voice sounded pleading.

I stood up and looked up at the door left ajar, even though I knew that even the slightest noise might have given me away – the wooden stairs sometimes creaked. I was feeling worse and worse, as if something was clenching my stomach, making me sick. I turned to go, ready to go down the stairs, but right then I heard the armchair again as someone stood up, and I bit my lips, scared and holding my breath, but I remained there as if I had been nailed down to the floor, unable to move. I heard something falling, but instead of running down the stairs, I climbed further up and stood outside the door. I heard a voice whispering, then gradually growing in strength.

"Come on, darling, let's go to the other room."

I wanted to run away, but instead, I abruptly pushed the door open and stood there without a word.

Harry's hand was in John's trousers when they both looked at me, startled. Their faces registered shock. John was the first to realize the absurdity of the situation, he looked down at his groin where Harry's hand seemed to be frozen in place, and yanked it out of there. His face looked like it was made of wax, his gray eyes were staring at me in horror, he slowly opened and closed his mouth a few times but no sound came out of it. Harry looked like he was feeling strangely satisfied with the situation and he bared his teeth in a grin, raising his eyebrows – at this moment, his face was like that of a comedian savouring the pleasure of the next scene. He gave me a contemptuous look and he turned to John. "Tell her, darling."

"Shut up!" John tried desperately to stop him, but he did not succeed, and the other man kept talking. I could not understand what he was saying – I was only seeing his lips moving and his face contorting. I abruptly turned and ran down the stairs – I thought I heard John's hoarse voice calling after me seconds before I left this house.

I sat in the car, fighting my growing panic, and I took two pills trying to control my breathing, but my heart would not stop slamming against my chest and echoing in my head. I opened the door of the car and let the winter cold embrace me, trying to concentrate on slow, deep breaths. I was struggling to keep what I had heard and seen out of my mind, repeating silently to myself, "Breathe slowly in... hold it... one, two, three, and slowly let it out – one, two, three". I do not know how long it all lasted, but at some point I felt the chill biting into my body and I felt better, so I started the car, drove to the next street and parked.

So this was the "X." from John's messages. It was not a woman but a man. I imagined the emaciated body of Harry in black garters and John ravishing him before he came to me in bed! No, I did not want to imagine it! I pinched myself to drive the nightmare away, but all I did was hurt myself. I was not dreaming – it was a nightmare come alive.

I was not sure that I was in a condition to drive – maybe I needed to leave the car somewhere and get a taxi. The drugs began to take effect and I was feeling somewhat calmer now as I sat and stared at nothing. The picture of my life, which had only yesterday seemed so ordinary, was now confusingly abstract. The more I looked at it, the more incomprehensible it seemed. I was feeling humiliated as I could still hear Harry's voice saying, "But we were together, even before you met Carina."

I had participated in this spectacle without even knowing about it, for years and years. My mind refused to accept it.

I had to get away, as soon as possible. I needed to escape to some place where I could empty my mind and fill my stomach. It was the only thing which could bring me some solace at this moment, however temporary.

I gave up on the taxi, started the car and drove. In the distance, I could see the traffic lights turn green and I stepped on the gas to reach them before they turned back to red. I had no idea where I was going. All I knew was that I did not want to go home or talk to anybody.

Traffic was light. A cigarette later, I discovered that I was near Warren Street Station. I thought about driving to Soho, but then I immediately remembered a small Italian restaurant close to the station, turned at the corner of the University Hospital and I was there in a minute. I walked in and took a table by the window.

While I was waiting for my food, I was busy analyzing what had happened and trying to picture the performance I had taken part in without knowing about it. So John had been cheating on me the whole time – now I understood why he had never told me that he loved me. And what about Margaret? Had she known about it all, and voluntarily agreed to participate? Because that lowlife John had been afraid to tell the truth about himself? Fearing for his career, or feeling ashamed, or both? How had he been able to live with the weight of this secret, and what had made him want to end his relationship?

There were many other questions in my mind, but if I kept thinking about it, I was going to explode, so I looked around to get my mind off things. I had missed the moment in which the waiter had brought me my food. I tasted it and immediately found out that it must have been longer than just a minute ago.

Later that night, I lay sleepless in my bed for hours. I did not feel like doing anything, and on the way home, I had not even passed by Daniel's house, like I did every day.

I was feeling empty and devastated – I was forcing myself to cry but I did not even have the strength for that. The sleeping pill which had become the lifeboat of my lonely nights betrayed me this time. Two hours and three pills later, my eyes were still searching the dark.

I was trying not to think about John, but it did not work. I was trying to calm myself with the thought that I did not love him, but this did not work, either. I got up and lit a cigarette, but in a little while, my stomach clenched into a ball and rose to my throat, and my heart started thumping against my chest once again. I looked around for my purse but I did not find it, and a moment later the panic drove me outside to my car where I kept some reserves of my pills in the glove compartment. My hands shaking, I rummaged inside it, but then I noticed my purse, grabbed it and dug into it. I took one pill, but I was only going to feel safe in the hospital at this moment, so I quickly made my way there.

❀ ❀ ❀

I was walking quickly and taking deep breaths to calm the beating of my heart. Or at least, I was trying to. I was one corner away from the safety of the hospital when I noticed a man's silhouette appear in front of me. I had no idea where he had come from, but I was certain that the street had been empty just a few seconds ago. Shivers of horror ran down my body when I saw him stop and slowly turn in my direction. My instincts were telling me that I was the reason he had stopped. I looked around at the nearby houses, but there were no signs of life in any of them, this early in the morning. I could not avoid the meeting, as I had almost reached the man, and here he was – the street lamps lit his face, our eyes met and the only thing I could get out of my mouth was, "You!", while my mind was screaming: *"Oh no, not you!"*

"Hello!" he said and gave me a look from head to toe before he continued without waiting for my reply, "Are you alright?"

Daniel's smile was quickly replaced by a look of sympathy.

I was staring back at him, aghast with surprise. If I could disappear like smoke in a fog, I would have, but I was not able to do that, so I kept shuffling in place, hectically thinking of a way to go as soon as possible, hoping he would not notice how bad I looked.

"Excuse me, but I have to go," I whispered, walking away in shivers.

"Are you really alright?" Daniel called out after me.

I was far enough now, so I stopped in the shadow of a minivan and turned back to him. Daniel was standing where he was, looking at me.

"I felt ill, I guess I'm too tired," I shot back with the lie. "I'll be fine."

"Are you alone? Are you going to the hospital?" Daniel looked around in surprise to make sure that I was really by myself. "Do you want me to come with you?"

Then he started walking towards me, without waiting for an answer.

"No!" I cried out. *"That's just what I need – Daniel knowing about my problems,"* I thought. "No, thank you, this is not necessary!" I added.

The determination in my voice gave him a pause. As he stood there, staring at me in confusion, I turned my back on him and quickly continued on my way to the emergency room.

The reassurance that I was in a safe place was usually enough to make me feel better. Once I had walked inside the hospital, I did not immediately need a doctor. For this reason, I did not go to the registration to check myself in. I had sat out the last few panic attacks in the waiting room, waiting for the crisis to go away by itself or attack me, but the latter never happened while I was here, so in an hour or two, I had quietly left, reassured that the panic attack had passed without serious consequences.

I felt uncomfortable with the emergency room staff because I often came here with my panic attacks and there was hardly anyone who did not recognize me. The first few times, they had invariably asked me if this had happened before, and I had been too ashamed to tell them the truth, so I had often replied "not quite". On the one hand, I was hoping that in this way, they were going to address my problem sooner, but on the other – I did not want them to know it was a panic attack, because they might not pay me any attention. And what if it was something serious, disguised as the symptoms of a panic attack, and they had sent me home without even examining me?

This time, it was different.

I forgot the reason for my coming to the hospital, I forgot that I had experienced a panic attack, as I sat there listening to my heart and my thoughts chasing each other, as if they were competing in their gallop.

I had planned on meeting Daniel, and carried out infinite imaginary dialogues with him, but when I really met him, it turned out that I had been unprepared for it. Meeting Daniel the way I looked – I gave a pathetic glance to the smiling teddy bear from the pyjamas I was wearing and imagined my nest of hair which had not been brushed since the day before, in addition to the dirty sneakers which completed my wretched looks – I could not believe my luck. I wanted to close my eyes and then open them to discover that it had all been a nightmare.

Maybe in the dark, he had not paid attention to the way I looked, may be had been just as surprised as I was – I was trying to reassure myself in my mind, even though I remembered very well how he had looked at me from head to toe when he had asked me if I was feeling alright. I was shaking with anger thinking about the impression I must have left Daniel with, anger with the helplessness the panic attacks made me feel and the way they restricted me.

"How are you?" A light touch on my shoulder made me turn in the direction of the voice, hoping that I was wrong, but the nice eyes which met mine were the living proof that my prayer had gone unanswered. While Daniel's eyes were searching my face, my mind was screaming, *"The hair, the pyjamas, no makeup this early in the morning!"*.

"Have you called someone to come?"

"Thank you for your concern, but this is none of your business," I snapped back, with an angry glance at him.

"I'd rather be alone right now, so I'm going to ask you to leave."

Daniel was startled to hear this; he raised his eyebrows and hesitated for a few seconds, then he stood up, gave me a look which said he was sorry, and said, "I just wanted to help you until your family comes."

My heart missed a few beats, but I did not let it show; I knew that he was speaking from his heart, but I just sat there and stared at him, adamantly.

"Get well soon!" he wished me, then he turned and left. I watched him walk away, and at this moment, I realized whom I had just forced to leave. I was flooded with hopelessness and despair, but I had no choice, I simply had no other choice.

I closed my eyes and hid my face in my hands, so that I would not see my dream go away. A slight fragrance of bergamot touched my nose and I felt like crying out after Daniel, but it was too late. I looked around – there was a woman sitting opposite me, using a handkerchief to dry the tears from her red face. For a moment, I forgot about my problems, I leaned in closer to her and asked, "Are you alright?"

The woman slowly looked up at me as if I was an annoying fly.

"It's none of your business!" she snapped and turned her back on me.

I felt crushed – though it was not the woman's fault but my own. After so many stressful situations, I needed some cleansing tears, but they must have been stressed as well, as they refused to come right now.

The excitement surrounding the encounter with Daniel and the pills I had taken suppressed my panic attack without the need for a doctor. My body was consumed with extreme exhaustion and I could have really used the bed's soft embrace. I stood up and slowly walked back home. After this cocktail of emotions, I needed sleep – and if there was such a thing as a forgetfulness pill, I would have taken two.

I woke up at seven in the evening after I had slept through the whole day. I lit a cigarette, took a large sip of my coffee and switched on my mobile phone with the hunch that there would be surprises waiting for me.

The first two messages in my voice mail sounded with Margaret's worried voice: "Carrie, where are you? Call me", "Carrie, call me, we need to talk." This urgency was not incidental – it only came to show that she knew what had happened with me and John. I wondered what part of the story she knew, and if she had known from the start. I refused to believe that it was possible for Margaret to have known about John and her husband all these years, silently accepting it all. There had not been even a hint from her that she had suspected something untoward going on in her family, and John had so many admirers at the university it was difficult to imagine he had been playing for the other side.

The third message was from John. I sat up, holding my breath to hear what explanation he was going to provide, but there was nothing of the sort. John just wanted me to call him, speaking in a dry, expressionless voice: "Call me, Carina." No apologies, no remorse – I hoped that he was not really thinking that I was going to call him, but then again, maybe this was precisely what he was hoping for.

The last message was from Margaret once again: "Carrie, are you alright? By all means call me."

This message only confirmed my suspicions.

*"John is gay."*

*"At least he's getting it up with you, while my man has a sausage instead of a cucumber!"*

Tina sent me the heart and smile icons, thinking this was the beginning of another "women discuss men" conversation, but the situation was serious and I was not in the mood for jokes.

*"I mean John really is gay!"* I repeated. *"I caught him in the act."*

After a short pause, my phone rang.

"Hello?" Her voice was worried. "What do you mean, you caught him in the act?"

"Last night at his place, he was with Margaret's husband – you know Margaret, the model."

"Were they having sex?"

"Not exactly, but I caught them with that guy's hand in John's pants."

"In his pants? I can't believe it!" Tina exclaimed. "You must feel terrible."

"I feel shocked and cheated, but I don't want to think and talk about John now – there's something else that..."

"What?" Lora asked, sounding concerned.

"Well..."

It took me almost half an hour to tell her about my encounter with John which had lasted for all of several minutes. Lora was listening with undisguised interest to my story, exclaiming "How could you!" every once in a while.

"I can't believe this is happening to me," I moaned desperately on the phone.

"You shouldn't have sent him away," Tina said reproachfully, sounding disappointed.

"I couldn't allow him to stay – I was in a crisis, my hair was a mess and I was swearing pyjamas with a teddy bear on the front."

"So what, he was going to see you like this sooner or later, wasn't he?"

"He won't," I declared sadly. "He won't even look at me anymore if we happen to meet."

"Call him right away and apologize. This way, you even have an excuse to invite him for a coffee."

"What if he says no?"

"Then he's gay."

We both laughed, then Tina busied herself advising me how to deal with the emotional crisis I had gotten myself into. Tina was always able to find the bright side of any situation and make me laugh when I was feeling sad.

"So call him and then call me to tell me all about it."

I promised her to do that – even though I was not sure that I would be able to.

❀ ❀ ❀

On Monday morning, I rode the train to Sarah's office. Over the weekend, John called and left messages in my voice mail for a total of exactly two times: one on Saturday night and one on Sunday. Both calls were at precisely eight o'clock in the evening and the messages said "Call me", the second one with a side dish of "Please". Margaret stopped leaving me voice messages but kept up the bombardment with texts, the last of which sounded ominous: *"Call me or I'll come to your place." "Thanks for the warning,"* I said to myself as I was reading it.

It was past ten o'clock when I arrived at Tower Hill Station. I walked out and took a turn on Trinity Boulevard, where Sarah's office was in one of the buildings along the boulevard. I walked up to the third floor and entered a large space with several desks with computers on each one. At first, I thought there was no one there, but then something in blue and rose stirred behind a computer screen and a smiling face appeared – the blue and the rose were two buns carefully shaped like little horns on their owner's head.

"You must be Carina, right?"

"Yes," I replied, a little perplexed.

"I'm Amy," my future colleague introduced herself and stood up to shake my hand. "And this," she pointed to one of the desks, "is Phil, our editor."

I was still trying to see where "this" was, when a skinny blondish young man stood up, waved in greeting and hid himself back behind the screen.

"He's not the friendly type," Amy informed me, as if she had read my mind.

"Come, Sarah's expecting you," she added and led

me through the corridor connecting the space to Sarah's office. "Tell me you're not working from home?"

"I am."

"You too? So I'll still be alone here – it's so boring!"

"You're not alone – our editor's here, right?"

"That bore!" Amy said with a roll of her eyes.

"I can hear you," we heard Phil's voice saying.

"I don't care, you bore."

I raised my eyebrows and smiled at Amy who rolled her eyes in Phil's direction and said, "He should be in the Guinness Book of Records for the most boring man ever. It's very seldom that he comes to the Friday parties."

"The new colleague!" Amy shouted out, peering in one of the doors.

"Come in and welcome!" Sarah greeted me. "Did you have a chance to look around?"

"Not yet."

"Amy will show you everything. She can be a real nuisance sometimes, but you'll never get bored with her, that's guaranteed."

"I heard something about Friday parties," I said, studying Sarah's office.

"Yes. Amy organizes them – every last Friday of the month, we meet in a pub somewhere, and this month we'll be expecting you – it's a chance to meet the rest of the team."

"Is there a lot of us?"

"No, but you're the best," Sarah informed me, with undisguised pride.

"I don't doubt it."

"It's only Amy and Phil who work from here, most people in the office are like you and prefer to write from home, but we'll talk about it some other time. Sit down – do you have any questions about the contract?"

"None," I replied, still looking around Sarah's office. The wall behind her back caught my attention. Her diplomas were displayed there in thin gold frames – one could tell that she was very proud of them and anyone sitting opposite her was guaranteed to see them and be reminded that she was not just Sarah but Sarah Hirsch Bradley.

I smiled at her and took the contract she had emailed me beforehand out of my purse, then I gave it to her.

"It's signed, isn't it?" Sarah asked me in a business-like manner, leafing through the pages. "It's important for me to have a signed contract for collaboration with everyone who works here. We also have an ethical code – I'll send it later to your email."

I had no doubt that she had an ethical code, as well – Sarah was a professional and her goals hardly knew any boundaries.

"So you want to be the new Murdoch?" I said to her in jest.

Sarah gave me a thoughtful look, as if she was calculating something in her mind.

"No, I don't want to be the new Murdoch or any other from the big five – my style is different, the time we work in now is different. I don't compete and I don't imitate – I'm something else, I'm Sarah Bradley. Now you'll have the opportunity to see up closer the way I work."

"Sure."

"We published the articles you sent us," Sarah turned her computer screen towards me as she spoke. "There are a few hundred comments under each one of them – people are very interested in your stuff. Read them and take a look around – I have a meeting with an advertiser and I need to go now, but I hope we'll have lunch together soon."

I had not even managed to open my mouth to reply

when Sarah had already gone out. I stood up and followed her – I had no pressing wish to know what people thought of any particular political event.

"Are you leaving already?" Amy grinned at me. "No one leaves without a promise they'll come to the Friday party."

"Which Friday is that?" I asked, even though I knew the answer.

"The last Friday of the month, but I'm asking you out for a drink this Friday. This way we'll get to know each other better, what do you say? Sarah tells me you like to party."

"You don't know what you're getting into," Phil spoke up, "she can be very obsessive."

"Shut up, Bore! Somebody asked what you thought?" Amy snapped at him.

I wanted to, but I hesitated before I replied.

"I'm not sure if I'll be able to make it."

Amy looked at me, puzzled.

"And when will you know for sure?"

"On Friday morning."

"Alright then, by all means call me. Do you want me to show you around the office?"

"I think I've seen enough," I replied with a smile. Plus, the depression had killed all my desires, but no one needed to know that. Well, not all of them – there was one left.

"Let me guess, you're in a hurry, right?"

"I have a date with the shops," I admitted with a smile.

"Wow, I love those dates – so have fun if you can, I'll devote myself to my work and it's a good thing I have it, otherwise I'd have died of boredom here," Amy said, raising her voice a little, probably so that Phil could hear.

84

"OK, I'm leaving you two love birds now," I said to Amy and Phil on my way out.

"Who, us?" the two of them cried out, almost in unison, before Amy added, "Let his wife love him, I don't."

I liked Amy's casual and easygoing manner – it seemed that she was having fun the same way she was communicating. As for me, I was not certain that I would be able to keep any promise, even if it was to meet someone in an hour's time, because I had no way to be sure that the panic attacks would not get in the way. I checked in my purse once again for my bottle of water and my medicines, and once I was reassured they were there, I made my way to Oxford Street for a post-Christmas shopping session. Margaret seemed to guess that I was about to sprint through her favourite shops, because she sent me yet another message, but I did not read it – I just switched off the sound of my phone and walked down to the underground.

The New Year sales were tempting and every shop was trying to seduce me with sales offers. As I was walking around and browsing the sales, my eyes were drawn to an evening dress, daringly open at the back and pleated at the front, with a golden necklace at the neckline. Looking at the dress, I imagined Daniel placing his hand on my bare back and the flesh between my thighs began to pulsate.

"Do you need any help?" the saleswoman's voice startled me.

"This will wake up male hormones, won't it?" I asked her, pointing at the dress.

She made a serious face, then she laughed, "It will give them a good shake."

We glanced at each other and burst out laughing.

"It's like it was made for you," she assured me, with

an approving look. "It will accentuate every curve in your body and you'll have crowds of men following you."

"I don't want crowds, just one. But you convinced me, I'm taking it."

I paid for my dress, continued shopping for shoes and got myself a few pairs, then I selected two blouses as well, and only stopped shopping when I realized that I would not be able to carry my bags.

When I got home, I ordered a large pizza.

❀ ❀ ❀

Later that day, as I was sitting on the couch in the living room, finishing the last remaining piece of the pizza, I decided to call Tina. I saw her online on Facebook and called her on Messenger.

"Hello," Tina answered almost immediately, but her voice sounded somehow different.

"Are you alright?" I asked her right away.

"No, but I don't feel like talking about it now. You'd better tell me if you called yet."

"Called who?"

"Don't pretend like you don't know who," Tina snapped at me. "You haven't, have you? Call him right now."

"I can't," I said, glancing at my watch. "It's almost seven o'clock in the evening here, and I only have his office number – I doubt he's working that late."

"How do you know he's not? Call him and then call me to tell me how it went."

"I'll call tomorrow."

"No postponing it for tomorrow, call now!" Tina turned off Messenger without waiting for me to say no.

I left the phone and went into the kitchen to make some coffee. Watching the brown liquid slowly filling my cup, I felt as if the coffee aroma was beginning to relieve the stress from my body and affect my brain. Even before I had taken a sip from the life-giving liquid, I could already feel its power.

*"Why not,"* I thought, going back to the living room to get my phone. *"I can call him, I'll do it."*

I lit a cigarette, switched off the coffee machine and searched online for Daniel's company once again. It was not difficult – I was just a few clicks away from dialling Daniel's number. There was hardly a chance of anyone picking up the phone so late, but it was worth a try – it is easier calling someone you are going to have a difficult conversation with when you do not expect them to answer the call than knowing the person on the other side is going to pick up immediately.

"Yes, it's architect Daniel Vasilev speaking," Daniel's voice sounded from the phone unexpectedly. I was not prepared to talk to him and I just stared at the phone without saying a word. Slowly, holding my breath, as if someone could see me, I pressed the red button. I stood staring at the display of my phone until it went dark and switched itself off. It was only then that I allowed myself to inhale. And right at this moment, the phone in my hand came alive.

"Yes," I answered without thinking about it.

"I just got a call from this number a minute ago, but it seems that the connection was broken." It was once again Daniel's voice.

"Yes, I... I'm Carina... John's girlfriend, we met yesterday morning, I found your number online and... well, what I did yesterday was very unkind and I wanted to apologize and... and..."

There was an inviting "yes" on the other side as I was searching for the appropriate thing to say. Fearing that I was about to lose the initiative, I simply said, "I want to invite you to have a cup of coffee with me, to make up for my unkind attitude to you. Are you free on Saturday?"

I was rushing the words out, before my hesitation had got the better of me.

"I'll gladly accept your invitation."

The fact that he agreed and his gentle voice helped me get over my nerves, and I bravely asked him, "How about four o'clock on Saturday?"

"Am or pm?"

"Let's say in the afternoon," I laughed at Daniel's joke.

"Do you know the French cafe near Hampstead Park?"

"In the house by the paved street?"

"Yes, that one. So we'll find each other," Daniel said cheerfully.

"See you at 4 on Saturday, then."

"Have a good week," Daniel wished me.

"You too."

I hung up and shouted out "Yes!", then I happily grabbed Poppy who was napping, and placed a kiss on his mug. Startled out of his nap, he quickly brightened up and mistakenly took my kiss for an invitation to play, happily wagging his tail.

"Not now, Poppy, I need to make some calls first, and then we're off to the park."

Trembling with excitement, I lit a cigarette and called Tina. I listened to the signal for some time before it changed to indicate that the number was busy. What was she up to? I made short work of two more cigarettes and took an aimless and restless walk around the room to give Tina enough time to come back online, then I tried again. This time, her reaction was almost immediate.

"I called," I informed Tina, my voice seemingly expressionless.

"You called, you let it ring once and hung up, or you called, let it ring several times and only then you hung up?" I could not miss Tina's sarcastic tone of voice.

"Is everything alright?"

"No, but I already told you that I don't want to talk about me, so you'd better tell me what happened," Tina

89

said with a sigh.

"I called, he picked up and I hung up immediately."

"You hung up on him!" Lora cried out. "Why do you even call him if you won't talk to him?"

"I didn't expect him to answer and I wasn't prepared for a conversation with him."

"So now what? Is that all? It's over before it's begun?"

"He returned my call and now I have a date with him."

"So the clouds are dispersing? That's great!"

"Let's not get ahead of ourselves."

"You're right, with our luck," Tina said with a sad sigh.

"This is the second time you're sighing tonight, do you want to tell me what's going on?" I asked Tina, concerned.

"Some other time, I don't want to upset you."

"Alright, you decide when, I'm always here for you. Peter called me, all of a sudden – he had seen my articles and he pretended that he wanted to congratulate me, but his intentions were quite different."

"Like what? Don't tell me he knows about you and John?"

"No, in fact I don't know if he knows, he didn't show it in any way, but," I raised my voice, "he wanted to have your phone number."

"He did?" Tina exclaimed, surprised.

"Yes, he was very insistent and..."

"And you gave it to him," Tina guessed.

"Yes, and I'll be waiting for you to tell me what Mr Always-in-a-Hurry wants."

"And I'll be waiting for you to tell me about Daniel."

I grabbed my umbrella and called out to Poppy that

we were going out. It was all Poppy needed to hear before he slipped between me and the open door and rushed down the stairs. We both did not care that it was cold and drizzling outside. I gave Poppy a smile, he looked back at me happily and dashed off to sniff at the trees and mark them. I followed him, full of energy, charged by the new emotions exciting my mind. Just remembering them, I felt a pulsating warmth in my solar plexus, even though it was accompanied by the fear of another panic attack. The image of Daniel's muscular body overcame it and made me smile happily.

"Carina, Carrie..." I heard someone calling my name and hurried steps approaching me from behind. I turned, abruptly.

"Carina..."

"John!"

My face froze in a twisted smile. What I had least expected and wanted had caught up with me – our last meeting and the inevitable final conversation. I knew that he owed me an explanation, but I did not feel ready to hear it, and I doubted that I ever would. Sometimes, things are best left as they are. Even the most fragrant and juicy fruit starts to rot if you do not eat it on time, or you do not like the taste of it for some reason. But it is better to leave it until it rots completely instead of poking around in it – the sight and the smell would make it even more disgusting and ugly.

I was standing opposite John, trying to determine what I was feeling for him right now. Anger, hate, sorrow... sorrow... No, it was not sorrow. There were no feelings at all. Nothing, I felt nothing. Absolutely nothing.

John was standing still, looking at me. I lit a cigarette and the bluish smoke clouded between us. For the first time, he did not object to my smoking in his presence. We stood and looked at each other. Poppy decided to break the agonizing silence with across whimper, objecting that his walk had been paused so abruptly.

"I'm so sorry, I can't describe the pain that I feel because of what happened." Gone was John's self-confident voice. It was only now that I noticed John had several days' worth of stubble, the lines on his face seemed deeper and his eyes were painfully hollow.

"I did not plan it to go like this."

"And how did you plan it to go, John?" I asked him ironically, but I was instantly sorry about that. "You know what, I think that I don't want to know what your intentions are. I don't care about them and I don't care about you, so how about you get out of my way immediately! Right now!" I tried to keep my voice firm and my gaze expressionless, and I think that I succeeded. John seemed surprised by my reaction. What had he been expecting, anyway?

"Carrie, let's go to my place and talk. I, I... I made a mistake, a huge mistake, I didn't want to hurt you and I know that we won't have it easy." John's eyes were searching my face. "We need to talk, I need to explain it all to you. I know it's not easy to accept it, and I don't know if you'll be able to forgive me, but, Carina, I really hope and I ask you to find the strength to do it."

"John," I interrupted his pathetic meanderings, "I don't feel the need to know! I'm not interested in your explanations, your excuses and your regrets. I'm not interested in you! If you worry about anyone finding out who John Roger really is, I promise that your manly dignity will not be blemished by me. Let's go home, Poppy!" I called out without even looking around for the dog. I walked by John and took off back home. John followed me and grabbed my hand. I sharply pulled myself out of his grip and gave him an expressionless look.

"Carina, I'm living with the thought of the pain that I caused you, I can't eat, I can't sleep, I can't work – all I do is sit and wait for you to return my calls. Believe me, this is killing me. Don't leave, give me a chance to explain everything to you, listen to me!" John struggled to swallow and stared at me, looking desperate. "No relationship is guaranteed to develop without crises, and ours does not make an exception. You have to listen to me, I know it's difficult, but you have to give me a chance."

"A chance?" I narrowed my eyes at him, but I quickly managed to control myself. "Look, John, I know that just now, I promised to protect your dignity, but if you keep insisting and bothering me with your presence, I'm not sure I'll be able to keep that promise. Stay away from me if you don't want me to make you the most famous gay professor in this country."

John was startled to hear this and glanced around awkwardly, his face drawn, before he attempted to say something else, but I beat him to it, leaned in a little towards him and ironically continued, "Don't disappoint your female students, John! And what about the faculty? I think they'll all be unpleasantly surprised to learn about you, John, just as I was."

John did not say anything in reply. He looked like his head was spinning. I bent down and picked up Poppy who bared his little teeth at John, snarled at him and cuddled against me. We took off back home, but after a few steps, I stopped and abruptly turned around.

"And before I forget, keep that bitch Margaret away from me, I don't want to see her!"

John was glued to his spot, standing there with the expressionless look of someone who had just been informed by his doctor that he was dying. He did not say a word as he gave me an empty look – I knew that he had heard me, but he did not react.

Exhausted, I made myself another coffee, lit a cigarette, lay down on the couch and let my emotions flow over me. I closed my eyes and told myself to think of Daniel. It did not work. John had intruded in my thoughts and he demanded to stay there. I had seen enough and experienced enough, the end of our relationship was inevitable. Somewhere along the way we had both followed, we had turned away from each other without knowing about it. This had happened so long ago that it was too late to search for a way back to us. And after what I had seen that night in John's home, it was also pointless. It was only now that I could understand his lack of interest for my nightlife with girlfriends and the lack of jealousy. John had called our relationship harmonious and I could not deny it, it had really been like that. He had never told me he loved me, but I always knew that he missed me when I was not with him. His fatherly concern for my career was touching, even though it was motivated by his ego.

We liked each other and we were convenient for each other, but everything happens when it needs to happen. It was over, it was all over.

In the next few days, I tried to write but it proved too difficult because I was overflowing with emotions. My thoughts kept coming back to the encounter with Daniel and there was nothing that could keep them on the subject of work. I could not sit still with excitement and worry about our first date. I went to sleep with Daniel's image in my mind and it was there when I woke up, I was thinking about him while I was writing and while I was eating, I was waiting impatiently for the day when we were going to meet and I kept pushing the fear of having a panic attack while I was with him back to the deepest corner of my mind. Each time the fear tried to impose itself on me, I was telling myself I was going to be alright.

And then it was Friday morning, and as I was frowning over my toast in the local cafe and wondering why I had ordered eggs on toast in the first place, Amy called.

"You haven't forgotten about today, have you?" she chirped into the phone merrily. "Three, four or five?"

"What, thousand?"

"O'clock, for now – we have to ask Sarah about the thousand, and we might even get a bonus."

"It never hurts to dream. Isn't three o'clock a little early?"

"The earlier the better. This way, we can have fun longer, right?"

"Let's make it four."

"Good, this way we'll have a chance to get a bite before we check out the fauna."

"Did you say the fauna?"

"You heard right, see you later."

"See you later."

I glanced once again at the slightly burned eggs, covered them with the toast to hide them from my sight and pushed them to the corner of the table. I took out my laptop and tried to concentrate on my unfinished article, but it did not work. Two hours later, I had begun several articles and I had not finished a single one – but on the other hand, I had already decided on the dress, shoes and coat I was going to wear for the date with Daniel on the next day. So what, Phil was going to give my article a polish – that was his job, after all, I reassured myself on the way home. Despite the freezing cold, I was feeling full of energy. I suddenly remembered that if Lora had been here, she would have called it "a dog's cold" – I had no idea why it was called like that and what dogs had to do with cold weather in the first place, but I was going to find out – I only had to remember to ask her next time we talked. At this moment, I was reminded of her unusual behaviour last night. What had happened? When was she going to tell me?

A few hours later, we were standing outside one of the pubs near the office, smoking with Amy, Phil and Marcello – a guy from work I had just met. In fact, it was just me and Amy smoking while the men were patiently waiting for us so we could go in together.

"How can you stand outside in the cold and smoke like that? Go in at once!" Sarah commanded us on her way in, not even slowing down before she entered the pub.

Half an hour later, it was her turn once again to leave first, after she had used her tablet to check out the competing news websites, even though this had not prevented her from following the conversation around the table and saying something every once in a while. After Sarah had left, Phil was suddenly eager to leave as well.

"Let's hope you're not as serious at home as you are at work," Amy said, watching Phil put his coat on. "There goes the last representative of the fauna," she added when she saw Marcello reach for his scarf as well.

"I'm sure that two beautiful representatives of the flora such as yourselves will be immediately sniffed out by some stud," Marcello replied, trying to match Amy's tone, but she kept her ground.

"Sniffing out is not enough, one needs fertilizing as well!" she said, then she turned to me and pointed with her eyes to the exit of the pub and Marcello making his escape, waving goodbye. "Doesn't this one look like a bonobo to you?"

"Who?"

"Marcello."

"Bonobo must be a representative of the fauna, but you'll have to remind me."

"Bonobos are apes – our closest relatives, genetically speaking. What's interesting about them is that they use sex to solve their problems. Plus, they're the only animals who use their tongue when they kiss each other, they have sexual intercourse face to face and they like oral sex."

"That's interesting. I didn't know it. But what does it have to do with Marcello?"

"He's told me some things – it doesn't matter, but I noticed he kept visual contact with your breasts more than your eyes, and for some reason, I decided he looks like a bonobo. What about you, have you forgotten your cheer back home?" Amy gave me a long look, like she was only now seeing me for the first time, and demonstrated an impeccable sensibility. "Problems in paradise?"

"I have a subscription."

"It's always like this with men – they were born to create problems and they're never around when you need them most. And then, they're wondering how come we're always depressed."

"You sound like a shrink," I laughed.

"And you look like you need one. Beer or wine?" Amy offered.

"Hmmm." I was hesitant about the safety of switching from my shake to wine, but then I decided that the antidepressants were a few hours' time away from the wine and I ordered with confidence.

The bar was already crowded and Amy took some time before she brought me my glass of wine.

"Let's drink to the evil we can't live without."

"Let's drink to the fauna."

"You can tell me," Amy offered. "Rest assured that I'm..." Amy did not finish the sentence but she made an "X" sign in front of her lips to assure me that my secret would be safe.

She did not need to tell me twice – I needed someone to unload my emotional baggage onto, and Amy was willing to take it.

"I broke up with my boyfriend, but that's not important. It's more important that I chased away a man I really like."

"If you like him, why have you been so bad with the guy?" Amy asked curiously, sounding almost drunk.

"Because I had no makeup on, my hair was a mess and I was wearing pyjamas."

"Oh, so you were drunk?" As if this was the only possible explanation for my behaviour. "And now you're depressed?"

Then she leaned in closer to me and asked, "How long has it been since you've had sex?"

"Do I need to answer that question? You're forcing me to think."

"There, I knew it that it's not you who's depressed, it's your vagina!" Amy cried out and the men on the next table gave us a curious look. Amy noticed and waved hello to them, then she leaned back to me and confidently said, "It's a scientific fact that the vagina gets depressed when it has no sex, this affects your whole body and it's the reason you're feeling bad."

Amy picked up her glass and looked inside it, as if there was something interesting hidden there, then she abruptly reached out to clink the glass against mine.

"It's fucking and fucking only which is the best antidepressant."

❀ ❀ ❀

I was still haunted by the energy of Sarah who was able to motivate others not just with words but with her presence itself. Her enthusiasm at work was contagious. Each time we had a meeting, I was filled with an irresistible urge to write afterwards. It did not take me long to finish the next article, I paid the bill and left the cafe. It was raining outside, but I was smiling as I was thinking about the upcoming date – Daniel and I alone, one breath away. I trembled, but not from the cold.

Daniel was waiting outside the cafe, as we had agreed. He was wearing jeans and a jacket with a sweater under it, and he looked just as he did when I first met him at John's house. As soon as he saw me, his tense face was lit by a small smile.

"You cannot go unnoticed wherever you appear," Dan complimented me instead of saying hello.

"I'm completely ordinary," I assured him.

"I like modesty, but you don't need it," Dan whispered to me as he opened the door of the cafe for me.

"Do you want to sit downstairs or upstairs?" Daniel asked me. "It's quieter upstairs," he specified.

"Upstairs," I replied without hesitation.

"Good choice," Daniel agreed as we took the stairs leading up to the second floor. We looked around – it was just us on this floor. We picked a table by the window and sat down.

"How are you?" Daniel asked me, a little hesitantly.

"I'm fine, thank you," I assured him.

"How did you find me?" Dan asked, looking at me with curiosity.

"Your phone number and your name were printed in

the offer and in the project you've done for John."

"And how is the professor?"

"I don't know," I shrugged as I replied.

Dan gave me a look of surprise.

"We broke up," I explained.

"I'm sorry."

"It happens." It was the only thing I could come up with.

"So what do you do?" Daniel kept asking me.

"I'm a journalist."

"It's an interesting profession. You must be very busy?"

"Sometimes I am, yes."

"I'm an architect, but you already know that. A recently divorced architect." Daniel's face was lit up by a smile, bigger this time.

"You look like you're happy with that."

"It needed to happen, and if I'd still been married, perhaps I wouldn't be sitting here with you."

"Perhaps," I said, raising my eyebrows in a challenging manner. "Just don't tell me you're monogamous, but not that much."

"Yes, I'm monogamous, but it doesn't matter. The important thing is that we are here together today, you and I." Daniel was looking at me meaningfully.

His perfectly chiselled cheekbones and his full lips awakened my desire to be close with him.

I had thought that one pill to ease my nerves before the meeting would be enough to protect me from excessive emotions that I knew I would not be able to avoid any other way, but I had not expected that the pill was going to surrender to the rising passion. This was a threat to my equilibrium, and the caffein in the coffee the waitress placed in front of me was threatening my fragile emotional stability even further.

"Are you hungry?" Dan asked me as we followed the waitress retreating down the stairs with our eyes.

"This chicken is very delicious," without waiting for me to reply, Daniel leaned in closer to me, pointing out one of the dishes on the menu.

"No, but if you're hungry, you can order for yourself."

"Not yet. We might have dinner later. Do you like Italian cuisine?"

"It's my favourite," I replied, looking at Daniel who had closed the distance between us.

His mysterious smile and the fragrance of his perfume worked like an electrical current running through me. My mind quickly surrendered to the rising passion, and when our eyes met, Daniel gently pulled me closer and our lips merged, in a manner which felt somehow natural. I caressed his face with my fingertips, then I slowly moved them down to his neck and elicited a small sigh from his lips. The moment I buried my fingers in his hair, the wooden stairs below us creaked. A group of overexcited young people appeared and occupied all available space with their loud laughter.

We reluctantly pulled away from each other, with a disappointed look at the invaders.

"I moved too quickly, I'm sorry, but you're so irresistible," Dan whispered in my ear.

Breathless, I had not reply for him, so I just looked down, self-consciously.

"Let me make it up to you with dinner."

I pursed my lips and raised my eyebrows, pretending to think about his offer.

"Alright," I agreed after ten seconds of silence.

A little later, we were already sitting in the local Italian restaurant, ordering dinner.

Daniel's smile and the muscular body outlined by his thin sweater, playing with my imagination, made me feel light-headed. I did not know when we ordered and when we finished eating – what I remembered most clearly of all was entering the restaurant. The rest of it was hidden in a pink mist.

I remember Daniel's invitation to go to his place and my refusal, I remember his insistent gaze and the hot kiss under the icy rain pouring down on us.

It did not matter if I was shivering with the cold or with the passion – the only thing that mattered was the closeness of our bodies.

"Don't you prefer shivering at home?" Dan asked me, his eyes searching for mine in the darkness.

"Some other time," I declined the invitation, but not the meeting of our eyes.

"Good night!" Daniel said reluctantly, walking me to the front door.

"Good night to you, too," I replied and hurried to hide inside, before my emotions had overcome my mind and I had followed Daniel.

Later that night, while I was listening to music and aimlessly browsing online, I received the first message from him which started a texting session between us.

*"Thank you for a lovely evening!"*

*"You're welcome – so I'm excused for the other night."*

*"There's no need, I was the intruder."*

Even before I replied to this message, there came another.

*"How about dinner at my place tomorrow night? I'm a good cook."*

*"Don't forget about the dessert,"* I provoked him.

*"If you eat your dinner, you'll get a double serving of dessert,"* Dan promised me in his next message.

Mmm. My imagination dove into an ocean of foretasted emotions.

The need to share my experience was pressing and even though I knew Lora would be sleeping at this time of night, I described in detail my experiences with Dan on Messenger, so that she would have something interesting to read with her morning coffee.

On the next day, the sweet haze I was swimming in abruptly left me when I received a message from Margaret.

*"Carrie, please pick up the phone when I'm calling you. Allow me to explain, I owe you an apology, I don't want to..."* I did not read it until the end – I did not care anymore.

Poor Margaret, I could not be angry with her, even though I was convinced she had played her part in the performance from the very beginning. She had known, she had always known about her husband's affair with John, and she had skilfully covered for them. In a rare burst of sincerity, she had told me how she had come to London, following her big dream of becoming a model. She could not get a break, so she had to look for a job as a waitress or a salesgirl, in order to cover her constantly increasing expenses. And just when she was totally desperate, she met Harry. Even though he was much older, he kept courting her and seducing her with expensive gifts. Margaret did not have to think twice about it before she threw herself in his arms, and when he found out about her financial problems and invited her to move in with him, she did not hesitate before she accepted. A few months after they met, he asked her to marry him. She did not hesitate again before she said "yes". Right about this time, she was invited to participate in a fashion show and her career as a model took off. And the rest of it – the rest of it was on her own conscience. Margaret had just one friend, and she was the one she saw in the mirror every time she looked at herself.

Hm... So long, Margaret! So long, past!

I forgot about everything the moment Daniel opened the door of his house for me.

"Welcome." Nervous shivers ran down my body when I stepped in. His smile and his kiss did not help lessen the tension which had come over me. Dan seemed to sense how I felt.

"How about a glass of wine before dinner?" he offered.

"As long as it's shared."

In seconds, Dan was already handing a glass of wine to me.

"To chance!" he toasted.

"Does anything happen by chance?" I replied, the provocateur in me coming to life.

"Of course, just look at how many chance meetings we had before we started planning them."

Dan bit his lower lip in a sexy manner and my heart fluttered. I looked around for something to help me conceal its treacherous dance.

"Where were these taken?" I directed his attention away from me and to the photos lined on a chest of drawers.

"In Bulgaria. Do you know where it is?"

"Of course, I've even been there."

"You have?" Dan said in surprise.

"Yes, I have a friend there, a Bulgarian woman."

"And do you have any Bulgarian men as friends?"

"*I do now,*" I thought, but I feigned regret when I replied to him, "No, I don't."

"That's fine, because now you have a man... who's Bulgarian," Dan said with a conspiratorial smile.

"I do?" I said with pretend surprise.

"You do, he's standing right in front of you." He looked at me with half-closed eyes which seemed to paralyze my body, then he gently ran his hands up my shoulders, continued up my neck, took his face in them and, keeping his eyes on me, moved his lips closer to mine. I opened my lips and put my arms around his neck. The kiss was sweet and brief. Daniel pulled a little back before he said, "Dinner will get cold if we don't hurry."

I reluctantly agreed and let him take me to the table in the kitchen.

Daniel refilled our wine glasses and served tagliatelle. The steaming plates gave off a delicious aroma.

"*Bon appetit,*" Dan said and began to eat with undisguised appetite, twisting the tagliatelle around his fork.

"It's very delicious," I admitted after the first bite.

"I'm a good cook, but I'm not good with desserts."

"But you promised," I pouted.

"It hasn't even crossed my mind to break my promise, but I can't make desserts, so I bought one. Cheers!" The clink of crystal and the meaningful male gaze made my body tremble. I was not hungry – the only thing I needed was an ice-cold drink to cool down the sexual tension in my body.

After dinner, Dan served me chocolate mousse with coffee. I accepted both, even though I was not sure a fourth cup of coffee this day would do me well, and if the dangerous combination with my raging emotions would not neutralize the effect of the pills, throwing me back into the numbing grip of panic.

Daniel was looking at me as if he wanted to penetrate my soul, or maybe something else. His eyes never left me as he watched me pick up the cup of coffee and take a sip, then they followed me when I spooned a little from the chocolate mousse and lifted the spoon to my lips, and then he leaned in closer and kissed me gently before he pulled back and licked his lips. "It's chocolate and coffee and a light rosy aroma, isn't it?"

"What?" My head was spinning, unable to think.

"The taste of your lips, combined with your perfume?"

"What about it?"

"You smell like roses."

"Yes, and you smell like bergamot."

"That's right." Daniel waited for me to finish my mousse, then he took my hands and led me to the couch where he lay me down carefully and pressed his lips against mine in a breathtaking kiss. My body was not late to answer with treacherous signals. I gave a small moan when Dan's thirsty lips found my throat.

The couch was too small for both of us. Daniel seemed to read my mind as he stood up all of a sudden and reached out to me.

"Come," he invited me, his voice hoarse. Without a word, as if I was in a trance, I took his hand and let him take me to the bedroom.

The bed was bathed in a neon blue light. Daniel made me stop and stood behind me as he gently ran his hands up my arms. When he reached my shoulders, he swept my hair back and ran his tongue down my neck. My skin prickled as every fibre in my body ached to succumb to the overwhelming passion. I felt Dan's hands caressing my neck, then they found the zipper on my dress and slowly opened it. He gently slid my dress down my shoulders and let it fall to my feet. His sensitive fingers explored my back first before they moved on to my breasts, they caressed my hard nipples and a small moan escaped our lips. I was feeling his moist breath close to my face and his hard erection next to my body. It was driving me crazy. I abruptly turned to face him, our eyes met for a second, Daniel leaned down, picked me up and lay me on the bed, then he leaned over me, breathless, his eyes half-closed.

"You're irresistible," Dan said quietly to me, his lips trembling.

In reply, I reached for the belt in his jeans, but his hand stopped me.

"Slow down," he whispered, still leaning over me, exploring the curves of my body with his hands. Then he unhurriedly slid off my lace underwear, gently pushed his hands under my ass, raised it slightly and lifted my groin to his lips. I felt his warm tongue playfully descend on my pulsating clitoris, and his frisky fingers skilfully find their way to my burning vagina.

"No..." I moaned and buried my fingers in his hair. The quicker Daniel moved, the stronger my moans became, and finally they turned into a cry as my whole body was shaking with excitement.

"No, don't stop!" I screamed with pleasure, pressing his head against my body, until I was swept over by the powerful wave of a shattering orgasm.

I let Daniel's head go, lay back with outstretched arms and struggled to breathe, my eyes closed.

When I finally opened my eyes, I saw that Daniel had undressed and was on his knees in front of me. His muscular body exuded manliness, and my fetish – big and muscular thighs – exuded an unmistakably manly sex appeal.

The sight of his erect penis brought me several mini-orgasms which I experienced without feeling self-conscious about it, under his thirsty eyes, without being touched, and then with the help of his playful fingers.

Dan's brown eyes gave off a peculiar glow under the neon lighting. He was kissing my face as he penetrated me deeper and deeper, his moist breath was caressing my ear as he was whispering something to me, but the words did not reach my mind, fogged with desire. Our bodies were moving in harmony, Dan picked up the rhythm and I followed, he kissed me and his tongue slid into my mouth in a playful rhythm.

A few powerful thrusts later, our bodies shook with a mutual orgasm.

In seconds, we were lying next to each other, breathing fast.

Dan turned to look at me, reached out and pulled me to him. I rested my head on his shoulder and cuddled into him, filled with satisfaction, I closed my eyes and breathed in his aroma. Dan took my hand and laced his fingers with mine.

"I feel like the luckiest man in the world."

"Why?" I opened my eyes and looked up at him, curiously.

"Because I'm with you. Even in my most daring dreams, I hadn't imagined I'd see you again, or for something like this to happen with us."

"And I hadn't imagined I'd be naked in bed with you on the second date."

"In fact," Dan raised his head and rested it on his hand, "this is our seventh date, which might mean that we've postponed this here for too long." The last with a look to our naked bodies.

"The seventh?" I looked at him, puzzled. "I think

you're wrong."

"I'm not wrong," Dan said with a shake of his head. "We met twice in John's house, twice in the night when I ran into you and you went to the hospital, and then there were the two real and planned dates."

"Do all these count as dates?"

"Well, they were chance encounters, but we met nevertheless."

"Even if you count the encounters on the night in which I went to the hospital as two, it makes six, not seven, doesn't it?"

"You probably don't remember the first one," Dan reached to caress my face, gazing thoughtfully at me. I thought that I sensed some hesitation in his warm chocolate-coloured eyes, I reached with my hand and gently buried my fingers in his hair without taking my eyes off his. Dan gently pressed me against himself and his moist tongue first slid along my lips and then between them. His tongue was playfully going in and out of my mouth, I gave a small moan and I pressed my body against his, filled with expectation.

"What did you want to tell me about our first meeting, Dan?" I purred in his ear, full of excitement and curiosity.

"The first one?" he repeated, somewhat awkwardly, and pulled back. "Our first meeting was at the post office – I was waiting in line when you came in, you took out your phone and you started typing something on it, and I was just standing there looking at you. You must have noticed someone staring at you because you looked up at me, gave me a look with your irresistible blue eyes, an almost imperceptible smile, and then you busied yourself with your phone again. I walked out of there before you and while I was still thinking about a way to say hello, you walked out as well and turned in my direction. I noticed that you didn't have a purse on you and I decided that you live somewhere close."

"So you've stalked me?" I said, playfully raising my eyebrows.

"No, I haven't. You walked in my direction and... Well alright, I was curious about where you were going, but I haven't followed you, not at all."

"Are you sure?"

"Not anymore," Dan laughed.

"And?" I said with a questioning look at him.

"And," Dan replied, pulling me to himself, "here's the result, you and I together."

"I..."

"Shh, don't say anything now – all that matters is that we found each other. Let me enjoy your intoxicating body."

I closed my eyes and let the overwhelming passion offered to me by Dan's body fill me to the brim.

I had no idea when we fell asleep, but I suddenly woke up. Dan's arm was around my waist. I slowly moved it away and sat up. At the same moment, I was hit by a hot wave and I felt my heart pick up speed to a hectic rhythm. I was already short of breath. I stood up and rushed to the living room; my purse was on the floor, I opened it with shaking hands and took a Clonareks. I opened the window ajar and the freezing night air gave me icy shivers. The cold chased the warm waves away from my body and all of a sudden, I started shaking. My knees went weak and I felt like I was sinking. The panic was taking me over, clutching me by the throat, threatening to choke me. I sat down on the floor next to the window, naked and shivering.

"Are you alright?" Dan closed the window and knelt down next to me. "Shall I call for an ambulance?"

"No, I'll be better shortly."

"What's wrong? Come with me, try to relax." Dan held my hand and sat me down on the couch. "I'll be right back."

He left me and then came back with one of his t-shirts and a blanket. He made me put the t-shirt on and put the blanket around me. We sat on the couch, facing each other. Dan's worried eyes were searching my face, trying to find the reason which had brought me to this state.

"How can I help you? What's wrong?" His face was centimetres away from mine, his voice was soft and gentle. His burning breath seemed to caress my face and spread down into my body. He pulled me to himself and I lay my head on his chest, still shaking, listening to the reassuring beating of his heart. His hand was gently caressing my hair, making me feel calmer already. The t-shirt and the blanket warmed me.

I could have kept quiet about the truth, but I decided to share it, even at the risk of our first night together becoming our last.

"The doctors say it's nothing to worry about, but I'm experiencing it in a very dramatic way. I've been struggling with panic attacks which I've been getting for some time now, more and more often recently."

"How long have you been getting them?"

"About a year now."

Dan put his arms around my waist and gently pressed my body against his, giving me the sense of security.

"You're feeling calmer now, aren't you?"

"Yes," I replied, uncertainly.

"Can you walk, or shall I carry you?"

"Where?"

"To the bathroom – you need a hot shower and a massage, it's relaxing and you'll certainly enjoy it."

"Do you think?"

"Trust me."

Dan held me with the blanket around my shoulders and led me to the bathroom. He turned on the shower and pulled me to himself.

"We don't have to do anything, just let me hold you and let the water wash the stress away from you."

"Will it help?"

Dan nodded and took away the blanket's embrace to replace it with his own.

We stayed for a dozen minutes under the shower, holding each other, then I put Dan's t-shirt back on and we snuggled back into bed.

"Turn onto your belly, let me give you a massage and you should feel much better."

But it was exactly turning onto my belly that gave me the next attack. I turned back around and sat up. Dan was watching me, worried.

"Again?"

"Yes, I need to take a pill."

"Don't, try not to!"

Dan stood up from the bed and spread a blanket on the floor.

"Come," he urged me.

We sat down on the floor with our legs crossed, facing each other.

"You need to breathe deeply," Dan said, holding my hands. "Now take a deep breath, hold it and let it out slowly."

I followed his advice, even though I trusted the pills more than any breathing techniques. On my second attempt, Dan stopped me. "You're not breathing right, let me show you, watch me carefully."

Dan slowly breathed in, bulging out his belly, then he

slowly let the air back out. He explained to me that this was what they called "diaphragmatic breathing" – with the belly bulging out on the inhale.

"And you're doing just the opposite, tightening it in."

We spent the next half hour on the floor, breathing deeply, following his instructions. I did not need a second pill – the breathing and the exercises combined with Dan's responsiveness and calm made me feel much better and I returned to bed, feeling relaxed.

"It's better now, isn't it?"

"Yes, I think it is."

"Have you talked to a psychologist about your condition?"

"Yes, but it wasn't any help, just the opposite. It was getting worse while I was seeing him, and I decided to use the heavy artillery."

"What did the psychiatrist tell you?"

"Post-traumatic stress and depression."

"And he gave you pills?"

"And he gave me pills," I confirmed.

"It's good that you did that – very often these conditions don't go away without pharmaceutical help, and they might unlock hypochondria or claustrophobia." Dan's face seemed darker when I looked up at him.

"Hey, you're talking like a professional, are you hiding something?" I said, trying to make light of it, but his serious expression gave me a pause. "Have you...?" I stopped before I said the question out loud.

Dan began to rub his forehead with his palm, staring at the floor.

"Have you experienced panic attacks?" I asked him, surprised by his reaction.

"No, but I struggled with this condition for a few years."

"How come?" I gaped at him in surprise.

"My ex-wife was having panic attacks."

"Oh, I'm sorry. Did she get rid of them eventually?" I asked, a little reluctantly, even though I was not cure that I was doing the right thing.

"I don't know – it unlocked various phobias while we were together, and she kept drowning them in huge amounts of alcohol which gave her a brief reprieve from her fears – until at last, she did not let go of the bottle night and day."

"Is that why you broke up?" I asked Dan, my heart tight in my chest.

"She wanted us to, but let's not talk about her anymore. You're strong and you'll deal with it, and if you allow me, I'll be by your side on this difficult journey. Go on, lie down on your belly, let me give you a massage, and then try to sleep."

"I'm sorry about the inconvenience that I caused you," I said with a guilty look at Dan, turning on the bed the way he had instructed me.

"Never mind me, what matters now is you feeling well."

Dan smiled, kissed me gently on the cheek and began to move his hand up and down my back, applying slight pressure.

"Close your eyes and relax, don't think about anything and try to go to sleep."

I did as he said and soon, guided by his hypnotizing voice, I felt light and relaxed, as if an invisible magic blanket had covered me, and my body sank into a blissful daze.

❀ ❀ ❀

I woke up in a room flooded with light. I lay there until my mind slowly cleared from the sedatives, then I turned to the other half of the bed. It was empty. I pulled back the covers and made for the living room, my body slack. There was a note on the closed door – I stepped closer and read it, my heart beating fast. *"I hope you're feeling good now! Thank you for last night. XXX."*

Is that all – thank you and bye? Nothing like *"I'll call you, baby"* or *"You were incredible, I can't wait to see you again"*? Incredible – I laughed nervously to myself. I really was incredible, with my panic. My heart began to thump in my ears, my lips went dry, I urgently needed water and a new dose of sedative. I quickly took a pill from my purse, sat down on the couch and waited for the attack to pass. Then I got dressed and left Daniel's house.

As I walked home, I felt the anger begin to poison my mind. Why did the panic always choose the worst time to come? So much effort, and then a few minutes of panic attack which ruined it all. God, why did everything need to be so complicated? Did I want the impossible, wanting this man? What if he never called me again?

I felt a lump in my throat and a dull emptiness inside me. A sadness came over me and transformed into fear that what I had experienced with Daniel may never happen again. I felt the need to share what had happened with someone – and who better than Tina.

I glanced at my watch – it was past one o'clock in the afternoon. I did not know if it was convenient to call her at this time of day, but I dialled her number anyway, and my call went straight to voice mail. Tina was teaching in shifts in her school, and I had asked her several times which shift she was working, but right now, my memory proved unhelpful. I gave a resigned sigh. Tina was going to call me back when she saw the missed call.

Poppy met me at the door, with an accusing look at me. I picked him up and he huddled against me. I did not and could not stay home, and I was not able to work. Perhaps cheerful Amy could offer me a cure to heal the torments of my soul? I dialled her number.

"Hello?" she chirped into the phone.

"I was wondering if you feel like having coffee with someone from work who is in the throes of love."

"Come over, what are you waiting for?"

"I'll be with you in an hour."

I walked to the station, deep in thought. Poppy did not share my downcast mood and happily whimpered next to me. An hour later, Amy was already waiting for me, looking uncharacteristically worried.

"Say hello to a failure," I began right away.

Amy made a disappointed face. "What, no sex?"

"No, it's not that."

"If there was sex, nothing else matters."

"It does," I objected stubbornly.

"So what is the other thing – tell me about it, I can't wait to hear the spicy details."

"We had sex and then I felt sick."

Amy did not know about my panic attacks and she did not need to know, so I spared her the details of last night.

"You're fine now, aren't you?" she said, giving me a worried look.

"Yes, if you don't count the anxiety that what happened last night might prove a bad start."

"Oh, forget about it and enjoy life!" Amy lowered her voice, almost to a whisper. "Was the sex so earth-shattering that it made you feel sick?"

"I don't think it was the sex, but I felt very awkward about what happened with me. What if he doesn't call me again?"

"Trust me, this will not affect what happens with your relationship in the least. So tell me the details! Is he well-hung? How did he treat you? Was he nice? Or maybe perverted?" Amy kept asking me questions and barely waited to hear the reply before she hurried to ask the next one, while I was trying to be evasive in my answers. "Why do you worry that he's not going to call you? No man will be able to resist you. No man will be able to resist his primal instinct. Everything is permissible on the way to the final goal, even lies. Do you really need me to tell you that?" she added with a mischievous smile.

"So what are you hiding?" I asked her in turn. "Where are the parrot-coloured decorations in your hair?"

"I'll tell you, but let's not do it now."

"It's a man, isn't it?" I said with a sly wink at her. "This is the reason for the transformation, right?"

"That's right, but please don't ask me any more questions."

Amy had already bought me a coffee and our passion for cigarettes did not allow us to go inside, so we were shivering outside while we smoked. There was a cloud of bluish smoke around us and above us, and Amy kept repeating like a mantra, "He'll call you, you'll see. I'm sure he'll call you. Who wouldn't call you to see your full lips and emerald eyes? If I was a man..."

"Amy..."

"Haha," she chuckled and gave me a playful look. Then she transferred the same look to the backside of a well-muscled man passing by, and added, "I like a firm ass on a man, but I always end up with assholes who don't now what they want."

Even though Amy's company had cheered me up somewhat, work was calling, and Sarah was not one to accept excuses.

"Amy, do you know is Phil has a lot to do today?"

"He's always drowning in work, why?"

"I have a few unfinished articles due today on my computer, but I can't seem to find my concentration, so I was wondering if I could ask him to finish and edit them..."

"Well of course, send them to him and don't even think about it."

I said goodbye to Amy, picked up Poppy who had dozed off, and carried the sloth back home.

I opened the file with the articles and gave them a disinterested glance. I was not able to work, as the tension would not leave me alone. I dialled the office without a moment's hesitation.

"Phil, would you do me a favour?"

"May I guess?" he breathed out into the phone, sounding bored. "I need to edit something or finish something? Why am I even asking, I know that I don't have a choice."

"You're so perspicacious, you know that? Remind me to get you a chocolate bar next time."

"No way, I prefer an ice-cold beer."

"You'll have it."

"So you do want me to finish an article for you, don't you? Why else call?"

"Will you do it?"

"Right after I'm finished with "The Connection Between the Menstrual Cycle and the New Moon"."

"Is it a new moon today?"

"Today, tomorrow, does it matter? I'm always buried

under a ton of work."

"So this is why I'm stressed and tense – it's the new moon."

"How can one say no to you, you kind and gentle creatures? Send me the article."

"Ummm, it's not just one," I mumbled apologetically on the phone.

"How many are they?"

"A few – three or four, maybe five, I'm not sure."

"Sent them over, but let me tell you that I'm taking a few days off next time there's a new moon."

"Just try it, and see how Sarah sends you off to another galaxy." He did not get my joke and the connection was cut, after a brief "Aha".


I had just sent the file with the unfinished articles when my phone rang. It was Peter, and I did not feel like talking to him, but I had no choice. I wanted him to relieve me of my obligations to his paper, and I was waiting on the answer.

"Hello, Peter!"

"Carina, we need two more commentary articles from you and then you're free of all obligations to us," Peter informed me, without any preamble whatsoever.

"So you found someone to replace me?"

"Yes, I have someone in mind."

"Do I know him?" I said curiously.

"You'll know about it when the time is right." I thought I heard some sly notes in his voice, but he was right. I was going to know.

"Thank you for everything."

"I'm sorry about you and John," Peter blurted all of a sudden, and my stomach clenched into a ball. The thought of John was buried and put to sleep deep in my subconscious, and this reminder activated my peristalsis, but I tried to keep my cool as much as I could.

"They say time heals all wounds, right?"

"So how are things with you?" I asked him curiously, without waiting for an answer.

"I broke up with my fiancée as well, but there's nothing to heal. I'm enjoying everything which happens around me and with me. I'll be waiting for your articles."

"You'll have them."

He had hung up already. Look at that – so Peter was full of surprises, after all.

I played some music, but instead of relaxing me, it was making me even more nervous. I stopped it immediately. My mind was feverishly leafing through the events of last night. The reason for Dan's separation from his wife was like a signal light blinking above me. What if he decided it was not worth it getting involved in the same kind of problem once again? What if he never called me again, what if... I looked at my silent phone. It told me it was almost seven in the evening, and I still had no text, no call, nothing. A deep sorrow was tearing me up from the inside, my heart seemed to slow down its rhythm, I wanted to cry but I did not have the strength for it, I felt a fear freezing me, almost paralyzing my body. How could I fail in such a stupid way, by letting him see me during a crisis, and why did I even tell him the truth? I could have been less open about it, but no. How could I do that, what was I thinking, why did I not get dressed and rush out immediately, why did I stay, why did I not go home?

I could not stay in this house for one more second, I needed fresh air. The warmth and the quiet of the house were smothering me.

"Another walk, Poppy!" I called out and looked

around. Poppy darted in from the kitchen, licking off the remains of food from his mug. "Come on," I urged him, "we're going out!"

Poppy did not need to be told twice before he stood by the front door and happily scratched on it with his paw.

Poppy and I were taking a walk and I was clutching my phone, looking at the silent screen every once in a while. The wait seemed infinitely long, as if time had stopped. I had not noticed when it had started to rain – I was standing in the rain and waiting for Poppy to go out from under a car. He clearly did not like the rain which was getting stronger with each passing minute, and he was hiding behind the tyre, timidly glancing outside every once in a while.

It was already past seven o'clock in the evening – he should have finished work already, but there was still no call. *"He probably does not want to take a familiar path,"* I was thinking. *"Why would he get involved with someone like his ex-wife again?"* I bent down to pick up shivering Poppy, then we made our way back home. I could not stand still with worry. Should I look for salvation in a sleeping pill? What if he called while I was sleeping? I rejected the idea and looked at the phone to see the time, yet again – it was 7:30. There was no point in hoping anymore, after I had not even received a single text the whole day. At 7:45 I could not take it anymore and took a sedative pill before I succumbed to another panic attack. At about the same time, Tina called. I briefed her on what had happened and sobbed in the phone, "He's not going to call me."

"Don't rush to conclusions, maybe something happened. I'm sure it will be alright. I have a good feeling about you two."

Tina's reassuring voice did not have an effect on me. No one was able to understand how I was feeling, as if I was on another planet.

"Let's talk tomorrow," I said to Tina, trying to keep down the tears.

"Alright, but are you sure you don't want to chat now?"

"Yes. Goodnight," I said, taking into account the time zone difference, then I hung up.

Yet again, I glanced at the screen of my phone. It was past eight o'clock. I lit a cigarette and turned on the computer, with firm determination.

Shortly after I started getting panic attacks, the psychologist I was seeing then advised me to register in a support group for people who had experienced or were still struggling with panic attacks. I had not entered the forum in months, and even before that, I had never asked the members of the group for advice. I confined myself to reading the stories of people who had similar problems to mine.

Bravely hidden behind anonymity, this time I decided to share and ask for advice.

*"Hello, friends!"*

Waiting for someone to join the group chat, I browsed through the latest posts. There were several stories of people who had managed to overcome their fears and, after years of crises, succeeded in finding a way out and leading full lives. They were touching and optimistic, but... There is always a BUT, an obstacle, something to trip you, just like your excuse that you are not strong enough to deal with it or you are too weak to fight it. There is always a BUT.

*"Hello, friend! If you are looking for a shoulder to cry on, I am ready to offer mine. And I promise to wipe your tears on Messenger."*

*"No, but thanks anyway."*

*"You're welcome, I'd be happy to help if I can. But if you ask me, to find the only cure to any condition, we must turn to love. The power of love can heal our bodies and souls with a magic wand. Love with all your heart and you'll be free of all suffering."*

I gave thanks for the advice and tried to focus on the words of my virtual friend, but I had trouble finding my concentration. The phone buzzed and made me jump. It was a message from Tina. It was just a single question mark, checking to see if Dan had called me already. I replied with the emoticons of a crying face and a broken heart. Tina immediately gave me the following advice, so typical of her: *"So you call him."* But I would not even think about it. My ego would not allow me to do that.

It was past nine o'clock. It was late, too late for a phone call, unless it was agreed on beforehand. The phone buzzed again. It was another text, probably from Tina again. I lit a cigarette, telling myself smoking was relaxing me. I was exhausted with emotions and I needed Lora's cheerful advice, and since she had decided to be of help tonight, why say no? I picked up the phone, ready to reply to her, when my eyes fixed on the message. It was Daniel, asking me *"May I call you now?"* My heart seemed to pause for a moment, then it was rushing again. I opened the window and filled my lungs with the moist air, I repeated the exercise a few times and only then let my answering "yes" fly back to Dan. He called me immediately.

"Hello," I said, summoning all my strength to make my voice sound cheerful.

"How are you?"

I was certain that I detected a note of worry in his voice.

"I'm alright," I replied, trying to conceal the agitation which was making me shake.

"I know I can't apologize enough for today. I was terribly busy and I kept hoping I'd be alone for five minutes to call you, but I could never get them."

"You'll have to excuse me about last night as well, I didn't mean to upset you like this."

"I promise that you'll soon forget about it all."

"I'd like to."

"Trust me. Do you want me to come pick you up – we can order pizza and sweets, what do you say?"

"I had a taxing day, let's postpone it until tomorrow."

"Do I have a choice?"

"It seems that you don't."

"Alright," Dan agreed in a resigned manner. "Pizza and sweets will wait for tomorrow."


*"Dan called last night."* Reporting to Tina was the first thing I did when I woke up on the following morning. Tina called me right away.

"Tell me," she urged me.

"Oh alright, hold your horses," I said and kept quiet for a second, then I screamed into the phone, "I have a date with him tonight!"

"I knew it that he was busy or something had happened to him," Tina concluded. "Knowing you, you won't be able to sit still all day with excitement, will you?"

"Do you say that from experience? And what would you do if you had found yourself in a situation like mine yesterday?" I said to provoke Tina.

"I would have called him, or went to his place. You

know me – there's nothing to stop me. I'm a woman of action – it's not by chance that the word "spontaneity" is in the feminine gender in my language."

The phone disturbed my state of bliss. It was my mother.

"Hello, Mom!" I needed to sound cheerful, otherwise my mother would get worried about me and I would have to spend the evening with her and Dad.

"I'm worried about you. Ever since you broke up with John, you almost never call, you don't visit and you hurry to hang up whenever we call you."

"Oh, don't worry, Mom. I'm fine. I have a new job, I have more responsibilities and I'm busy."

"I know, I know. Come to our place for a while."

"What, to live with you?" I asked, puzzled.

"Yes. I don't want you to suffer," my caring mother moaned on the phone.

"I'm not suffering, Mum. As I matter of fact, I'm happy. I don't need to move in with you, but I promise I'll come see you soon."

"I hope so."

My mother tried to add something else, but I interrupted her. "Bye, Mum, I have a call on the other line and it's important – bye!"

Busy writing articles, smoking and daydreaming about Dan, I had not noticed the day go by.

"Outside or inside?"

"Mmm, give me a hint. Is there a correct answer?"

"Both. How about first we go to my place to order pizza and have dinner, and then we take a walk in the park?"

"It's a great idea! When do you get off work?"

"I can pick you up in an hour. Will you be ready by then?"

"It's quite enough. I'll see you then."

"I can't wait to see you."

"Me too," I replied, somewhat awkwardly, even though I wanted to say it at least three times: Me too, me too, me too.

Already dressed and wearing makeup, I was impatiently pacing my small place which seemed like a carton box now, and I could not wait to go out as soon as possible. I had no need of sedatives, but one could never be too careful, especially on a date with Dan. I could not allow myself to have another panic attack in his presence.

Ready and waiting, I sat down with a smoking cigarette in one hand and my phone in the other. Even teenagers in love probably managed to control their emotions better, but then again, I was happy – and no one should be blamed for feeling happy, should they?

"This is for you, with my apologies about yesterday," Dan said, taking out his hand from behind his back. He was holding a bouquet of roses.

"Oh, Dan, they're so beautiful and... thank you!" Speechless, I took the bouquet and I was about to kiss Dan when I noticed the golden reflections on the rose petals. I looked at the bouquet more carefully and opened one of the flowers.

"But, Dan, this is a bouquet of sweets, with my favourite chocolates in each rose. This is such a sweet gesture!" I exclaimed, melting with pleasure, looking into his enchanting eyes. "How can you know what my favourite chocolates are?"

"Intuition, darling. So am I excused for yesterday?"

"I can't forgive anything when I'm hungry," I purred in reply. "Make sure I'm full, and then I'll be more benevolent."

"You fox, let's go then," Dan said, throwing his arm over my shoulders and leading me to his place.

We arrived just in time. The pizza delivery guy was just ringing the bell. Dan grabbed the boxes and a little later, we were already attacking the pepperoni pizza with our fingers. I listened to Dan's advice to abstain from coffee, but I found it much more difficult to do without cigarettes.

"Do you want to take a walk in the park?" I began.

"Do you want to smoke?" Daniel laughed, and I nodded. "Let's go then."

Minutes later, we were already walking aimlessly through the park, holding hands. I was smoking and Dan was telling me about his life in Bulgaria and the decision to leave it and come to live in London. His story was intriguing and his voice was deep and calm.

"Has your Bulgarian friend ever taken you to the Black Sea coast?"

"Tina? No, she lives far away from the sea."

"You'll love it – golden sands and salty sea waves... I have experienced the most beautiful sunrises and sunsets in my life there, and wait till you see the night sky full of stars and the moon reflected in the waves – you will love this place, and you'll never again want to return to rainy London."

"Oh, Dan, it all sounds so romantic," I exclaimed, picturing us lying on the beach and staring at the night sky.

"In fact," Dan stopped and looked at me, "I'm taking

you to Bulgaria in the summer."

I did not say anything in reply – I let his lips gently touch my neck and his warm breath burn me from the inside.

Aglow after the walk, we ended up in bed. This time, it was me telling him about myself, while Dan was massaging my body. I was feeling calm and relaxed. Dan delicately turned the conversation to the subject of my panic attacks and I began to lay bare the truth about my condition, easily and without thinking about it too much. I also told him about the phobias which were unlocked in me shortly after the panic attacks began. Dan was listening carefully, without interrupting me with questions, lying next to me with his head on one hand and the other hand skillfully massaging my back. I went so far as to admit to him about the fear I felt whenever I had to ride the train through the tunnel from Hampstead Heath to Richmond.

"The one after Hampstead Heath?" Dan asked me, surprised, and sat up in bed.

"Yes, I feel panic that the train might stop right there, in that claustrophobic tunnel, and I wouldn't be able to get out and choke to death inside. I don't know how fast the train goes, but that minute it takes it to go through the tunnel is a nightmare, and if the train doesn't come out in a minute, I'll have a crisis which might be fatal for me."

I did not know if it was wise being so candid with my lover, but I had an irresistible urge to confide everything in him, including my fears. I wanted to be sincere with him, even if I felt sorry for it afterwards. I was hoping to disperse the leaden clouds darkening my days. Maybe I was going to succeed, with him. Maybe.

"Have you tried to overcome that fear?" Dan asked me, concerned.

"Yes, I avoid riding on that train."

"How about in a different way?"

"This is the best way – stay away from your fears."

"I read online about people suffering from panic attacks. The stories say that once you overcome the panic attacks, in most cases phobias disappear by themselves."

"I've tried almost everything," I said with a sigh.

Dan was slowly massaging me and it made me sleepy. I yawned and closed my eyes, ready to succumb to sleep, when he suddenly said, "I'm going to the gym at 6 am tomorrow and you'll come with me, right?"

"At six o'clock? Why so early, can't we go in the evening?"

"In the evening, I'm tired and hungry."

"I don't have anything to wear," I tried to excuse myself.

"Don't go looking for excuses, we'll go get your exercise outfit."

"Uh..."

At 5:30 in the morning, the phone alarm found me in bed, well snuggled next to Dan.

"It's time for the gym," Dan's cheerful voice boomed in my ear.

"Hmmm..."

"Don't purr now, come in the shower and you'll be all fresh in a minute!"

"M..."

"Come on, you're just a few metres away from the shower."

"Waking up at 5:30, the gym at 6, this is torture," I kept complaining, dragging my feet to the bathroom with my eyes half-closed. Suddenly, an icy stream of water hit my body and I screamed.

"If you complain like that again the next time, I'll wake you up with a cold shower again. Look at you now, you're more awake than ever. Come," he reached out to me and pulled me in under the shower, already warm.

The next few weeks passed by quickly. Dan and I went to the gym every day, then we had breakfast together and he went to work, and I sometimes sat down to write in his house and sometimes went back to mine. With a smile on my face, the writing was going good. I was smiling at the thought that we were mere hours away from being next to each other again.

In his delicate and unobtrusive way, Dan was making an effort to help me overcome my panic attacks, and he sincerely believed that I was going to succeed. Enchanted by the thrill of love, I realized there must have been whole days in which I had not even thought about the pills – Dan's fragrance, or the memory and expectation of Dan's fragrance, had been enough for me to forget about my need for them. The last time I discovered that I did not have the pills in my purse, I did not rush straight home like I always did when it turned out I had neglected to take them with me. I was hoping that I would never need them again, but... their presence in my purse was still reassuring.

Dan gave me a hot kiss and then he offered, "How about fish for dinner?"

"Alright, but don't expect me to cook it."

"No one's cooking, I'm taking you to a special place. They make the best fish and chips."

Dan was quiet for a moment before he added, "The restaurant is in West Hampstead and I'm thinking we can go on the train."

"The train? Why not take the car?"

Dan was staring at me, his usual smile gone from his

face, trying to look into my soul with his serious eyes.

"What?" I asked him, feeling icy shivers running down my body. "I thought we were going out to have dinner, not near-death experiences."

"I promise there won't be any," he replied, a mysterious smile on his face once again.

"Then let's take one of the cars and forget about the train," I said, lit by a beam of hope, but Dan's expression remained resolute.

He reached out to me and I took his hand like an obedient child. I let him lead me to Gospel Oak Station, one stop on the train before the tunnel.

"Why don't we get on the train at Hampstead Heath instead of using a station in the opposite direction?"

"You need time."

"You want to prolong my agony?" I pouted as we took the stairs to the platform.

"Not at all – I want you to have enough time to become aware of your fear."

"Did you think to ask me if I wanted to become aware of my fears right now, this evening? Shouldn't you have told me about your intentions, as they concern me, after all?"

Dan disregarded my protests which were probably about to escalate – instead, he kept his calm and continued, "What you're avoiding is what you need to direct your attention to. This fear is not real, and I want to show you, to prove to you, that there's nothing to be afraid of. There's only the fear of the fear itself."

"It's totally real for me..."

The train arrived and put a stop to our conversation. We boarded it, Dan looked around, found two empty seats next to each other and we sat down. He squeezed my hand and whispered, "Trust me. You're not getting a panic attack this time."

I looked at him – he seemed calm, but this did not reassure me. I felt hot, I was sweating, my jaw was locking, my tongue was sticky in my mouth. Dan was still holding my hand and I did not dare to turn to him, so that he would not see the panic rising in me. At this moment, the train stopped at Hampstead Heath and a fresh breath of air from the open doors caressed my face. I had no more than a minute to make the decision to get off the train and end this ordeal. I watched the closing train door, hypnotized. My heart was reverberating in my stomach, then in my head, I felt my legs go soft, and then I heard Dan's voice.

"Turn around and look," he stood up and turned to face the window, with his knee on the seat. I followed his example, all but paralyzed with fear. Dan put his hand on my shoulder and pulled me closer to the window. I followed him without a word, my mind in a haze, convinced that this was the end. The blood was pulsing in my veins and I was about to close my eyes, but Dan's kiss made me open them the moment the train entered the lit tunnel. It was the first time I was seeing the tunnel, well-lit and wide. It was not narrow in the least. There was another set of rails for the train in the opposite direction. Surprised by my discovery, I felt Dan's gaze on my face, and he seemed to guess at the emotions that I was experiencing right now, because he kissed me on the cheek. Then we turned and sat back on our seats. Dan was still holding my hand. My mind slowly cleared, the beating of my heart calmed down and I realized the absurd fallacy I had been suffering from. I turned to Dan, avoiding his eyes.

"It's stupid, isn't it?" I directed the question more at myself than at him. "It's unbelievable how many times I have travelled this route, and I've never realized that there must be two sets of rails and the tunnel can't be claustrophobically narrow. Once, when I was riding this train, I experienced a panic attack right at the moment in which the train entered the tunnel – it was dark and I was struggling with myself until I saw the light at the other end, I got off at the next stop and for a long time afterwards, I didn't dare to ride this train anymore, and when I decided to do it, the fear would freeze my mind as the train was approaching the tunnel."

"Sometimes, we're more inclined to obey our fear than our good sense, but you'll get over it sooner than you think."

"What makes you so sure?"

"Because you're taking the most powerful antidepressant there is, each morning."

"So you did it on purpose..." I did not finish the sentence when I saw him grinning.

Then I had another thought.

"Did you go to the gym before you met me?"

"Almost never, but then I had to."

"For me." I had no words to thank him.

"You can thank me properly when we get back home," Dan said, playfully raising his eyebrows. "In case you haven't noticed, we missed our stop a long time ago and if we want to eat any time soon, we'd better get off the train and take another one back."

Awkward and ashamed, but also filled with new feelings, I let Dan take me to the restaurant.

"You've forgotten, haven't you?" Amy's accusing voice came from the phone.

"Forgotten what?" I could not recall promising anything.

"The collegial meeting."

"You mean we have a team building session?"

"It's more like the dream team will have a dream drink."

"I wouldn't dare to miss such an event."

"Hey, this time your hair is red and braided!" I exclaimed when I saw the change in Amy.

"Do you like my braids?" she asked me cheerfully, touching them. Then she leapt up from her chair, gave me an excited look from head to toe before she hugged me, and smiled slyly as she concluded, "I can see love blossoming."

This time, Phil waved hello and told me that he was going to be free soon, without me even asking him about it. Right then, Sarah entered the office and turned to Amy. "Take off the rose-tinted glasses and finish your job before we leave."

Amy pretended to sulk and sat back down in front of her computer. Sarah and I entered her office and it was only then that she allowed herself to change the business-like expression on her face with a friendly smile, even though she continued talking business.

"Phil told me your articles don't need editing. You write fast and you write with style, but I recommend that you read the readers' comments – they are good for your self-confidence. And most importantly, keep up the good work. And as I won't be able to attend our meeting today – what or who do I have to thank for the change in you?"

"What is it, have I changed?"

"You look like someone happy with their life and I can see a sparkle in your eyes, so who's the lucky one?"

"It looks like it's me, but he's incredible."

"He's a magician, then. Well, enjoy him and don't lose your enthusiasm for work."

Just an hour after we had sat down in the local pub, it

was just me and Amy. Phil was the last one to leave and I thought I noticed him and Amy exchanging meaningful looks.

"I want details, pictures, is he in love with you, are you in love with him, tell me all about it," Amy urged me on, enthusiastically.

"I suggest we start with you – and Mr Bore. While he was sitting here pretending to be absent-minded, I could smell love pheromones, and do you know when they're emitted?"

Amy half-closed her eyes and pretended to be bashful.

"It turned out he was not so boring after all, but just like you, I suggest we talk about it after it's a fact."

"So you're superstitious – but it seems like that's not stopping you from throwing a playful glance or two at the representatives of the fauna."

Amy looked around at the male visitors in the pub, slowly and carefully, and came to a sad conclusion.

"All I see is uninteresting representatives of the fauna. It's so boring," she sighed.

"Wait a minute. The guy from work is married, isn't he?"

"Yes, he's still married, but we're not doing anyone any harm, we're just having some fun."

"But you're in love with him, admit it!"

"I don't know yet – I prefer not to think about my feelings."

"Oh, I see! Well, let's drink to love!"

Amy raised her beer mug and I raised my glass of orange juice.

❀ ❀ ❀

"I can't, Dan, I'm tired, why don't we go to the gym in the evening, just once?" I kept complaining, sitting on Dan's bed. "I'm sleepy, can't we postpone it? Look, I'm even unable to open my eyes," I turned my face to him, to show him how I was feeling.

"Come." Dan took me into his arms and pushed my hair from my face. "Are you very tired?"

"Can't you see?" I raised my face to him without opening my eyes.

"Are you fishing for sympathy, you fox?"

"No, just understanding," I replied in a drawl, but then I could not resist my curiosity and opened half an eye. Dan immediately caught me and we both laughed.

"Working out is very important for you, darling – the only way to raise endorphin levels is through exercise and laughter."

"It's not the only way, bananas are a source of endorphin as well. How about we take a bite instead of working out?"

"You're so full of temptations that I'll probably succumb to you, but first we need to go to the gym."

"You're providing enough serotonin for me and I feel healthy, the last panic attack I had was... I refuse to remember, but it was a long time ago."

Dan sighed. "We're staying in bed, but this is an exception and we mustn't make a habit out of it."

"Aha," I muttered and stuck my head in my favourite place, under Dan's arm. He kissed me and lay back next to me.

"Thank you! You're so devoted and caring."

"And I should thank you as well."

"You? What for?"

"You know what for."

"I don't – give me a hint."

"For the opportunity to be together with you."

"Darling, you're my three in one – a lover, a friend and a therapist."

"Am I the best?"

"You're the best multiplied by three!"

Dan leaned over me – his eyes were shining with a peculiar light and he was biting his lower lip in that enchanting way he had. Then he slightly opened his lips and before he kissed me, he quietly whispered, "We're two in one."

"I know and I love you, darling. I love you!"

"I love you too... Let's not fight over who loves the other one more."

TOXIC LOVER
*a novel*

Carrie Jan, *author*

Bogdan Rusev, *translator*
Petra Limosa, *graphic design*

Printed sheets 8,75
Format 84/108/32

First edition
ISBN 978-954-471-756-8

Libra Scorp Publishing House
www.meridian27.com

2021